TEEN TITANS GO!

STONE ARCH BOOKS™
Published in 2014
A Capstone Imprint
1710 Roe Crewst Drive
North Mankato, MN 56003
www.capstonepub.com

DC Comics
1700 Broadway, New York, NY 10019
A Warner Bros. Entertainment Company

Cataloging-in-Publication Data is available at the Library of Congress website:
ISBN: 978-1-4342-9213-1 (library binding)

Summary: Raven refers to her newest zit as a real monster--which proves to be quite literally the case when the blemish becomes an entity of its own! Follow Robin, Beast Boy, Cyborg, Raven, and Starfire as these teenage super heroes team up to take down super-villains and schoolwork alike.

STONE ARCH BOOKS
Ashley C. Andersen Zantop *Publisher*
Michael Dahl *Editorial Director*
Sean Tulien *Editor*
Heather Kindseth *Creative Director*
Alison Thiele *Designer*
Tori Abraham *Production Specialist*

DC COMICS
Lysa Hawkins & Tom Palmer Jr. Original U.S. Editors

Printed and bound in the USA.
009770R

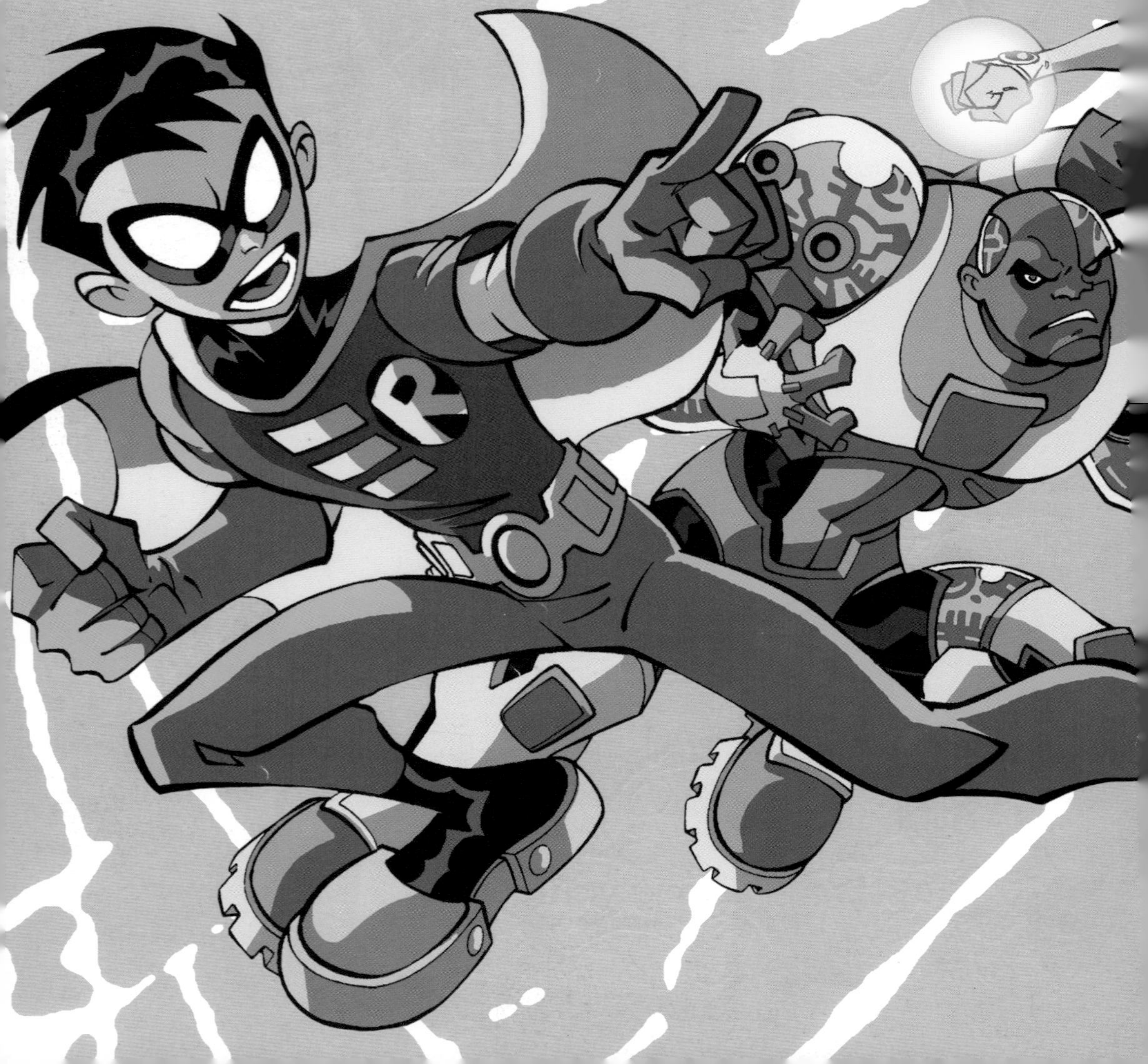

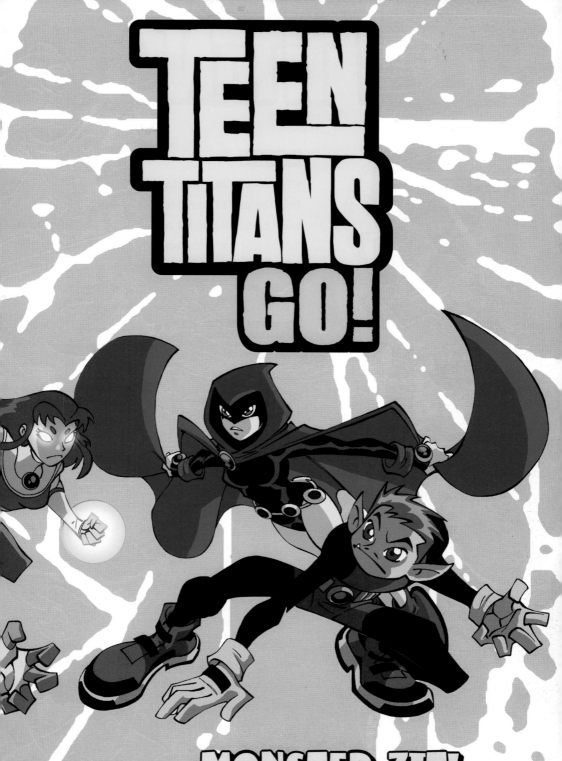

TEEN TITANS GO!

MONSTER ZIT!

J. Torres.. writer
Tim Smith III & Lary Stucker.....................artists
Heroic Age..., colorist
Jared K. Fletcher.................................. letterer

TEEN TITANS GO!

ROBIN

REAL NAME: Dick Grayson

BIO: The perfectionist leader of the group has one main complaint about his teammates: the other Titans just won't do what he says. As the partner of Batman, Robin is a talented acrobat, martial artist, and hacker.

STARFIRE

REAL NAME: Princess Koriand'r

BIO: Formerly a warrior Princess of the now-destroyed planet Tamaran, Starfire found a new home on Earth, and a new family in the Teen Titans.

CYBORG

REAL NAME: Victor Stone

BIO: Cyborg is a laid-back half teen, half robot who's more interested in eating pizza and playing video games than fighting crime.

RAVEN

REAL NAME: Raven

BIO: Raven is an Azarathian empath who can teleport and control her "soul-self," which can fight physically as well as act as Raven's eyes and ears away from her body.

BEAST BOY

REAL NAME: Garfield Logan

BIO: Beast Boy is Cyborg's best bud. He's a slightly dim but lovable loafer who can transform into all sorts of animals [when he's not too busy eating burritos and watching TV]. He's also a vegetarian.

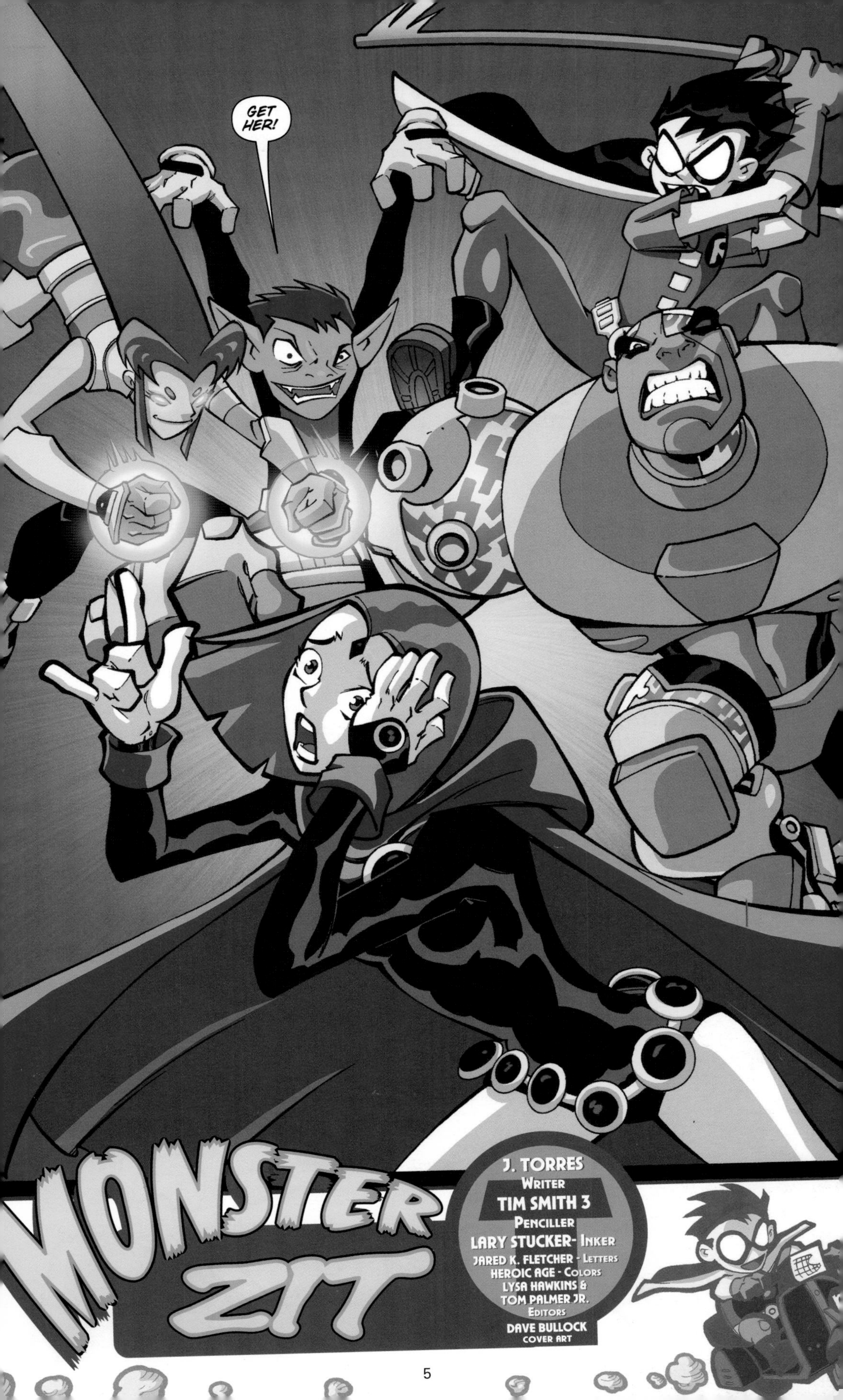
GET HER!
MONSTER ZIT
J. TORRES
Writer
TIM SMITH 3
Penciller
LARY STUCKER- Inker
JARED K. FLETCHER - Letters
HEROIC AGE - Colors
LYSA HAWKINS &
TOM PALMER JR.
Editors
DAVE BULLOCK
COVER ART

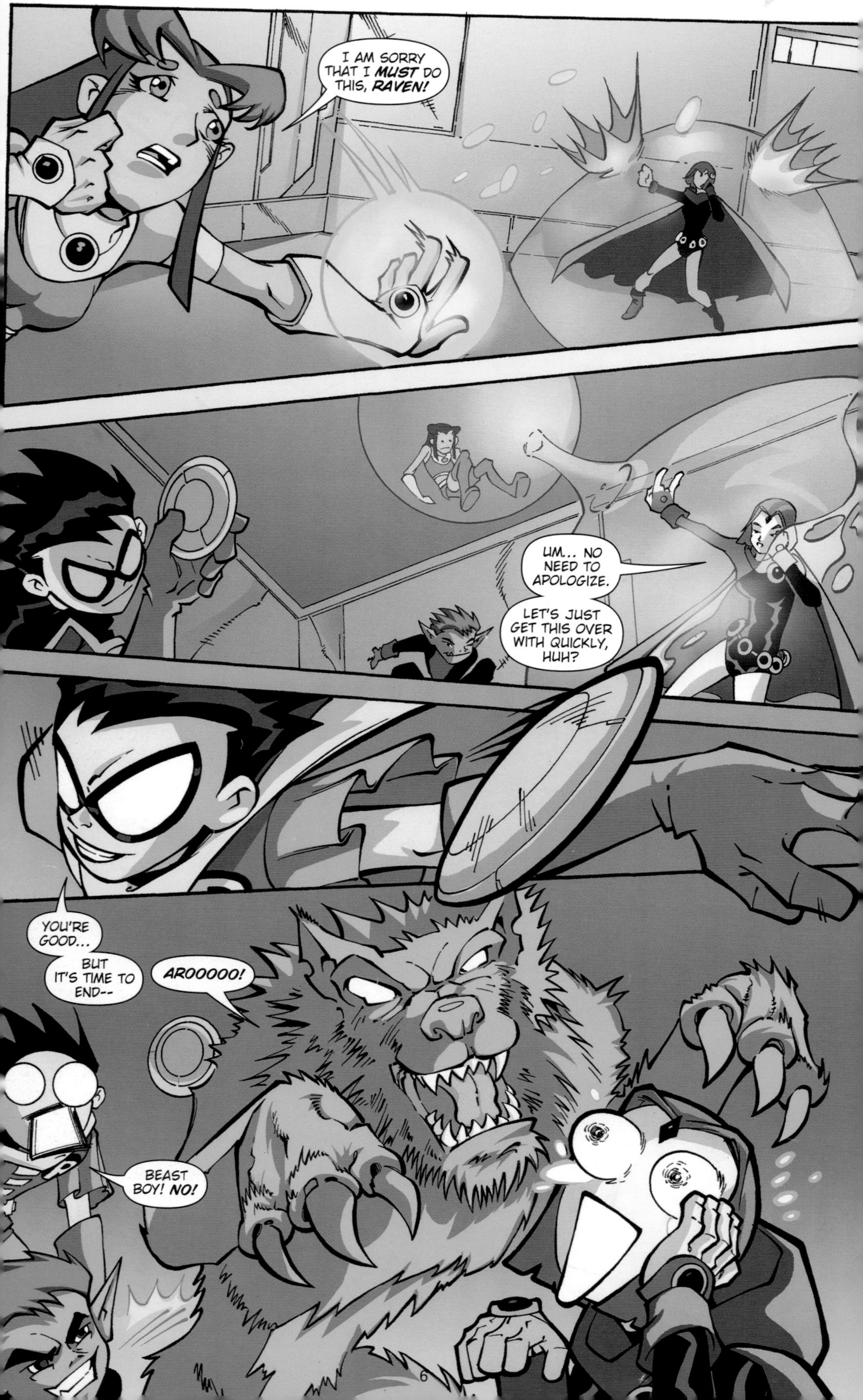
I AM SORRY THAT I **MUST** DO THIS, **RAVEN!**
UM... NO NEED TO APOLOGIZE.
LET'S JUST GET THIS OVER WITH QUICKLY, HUH?
YOU'RE GOOD...
BUT IT'S TIME TO END--
AROOOOO!
BEAST BOY! **NO!**

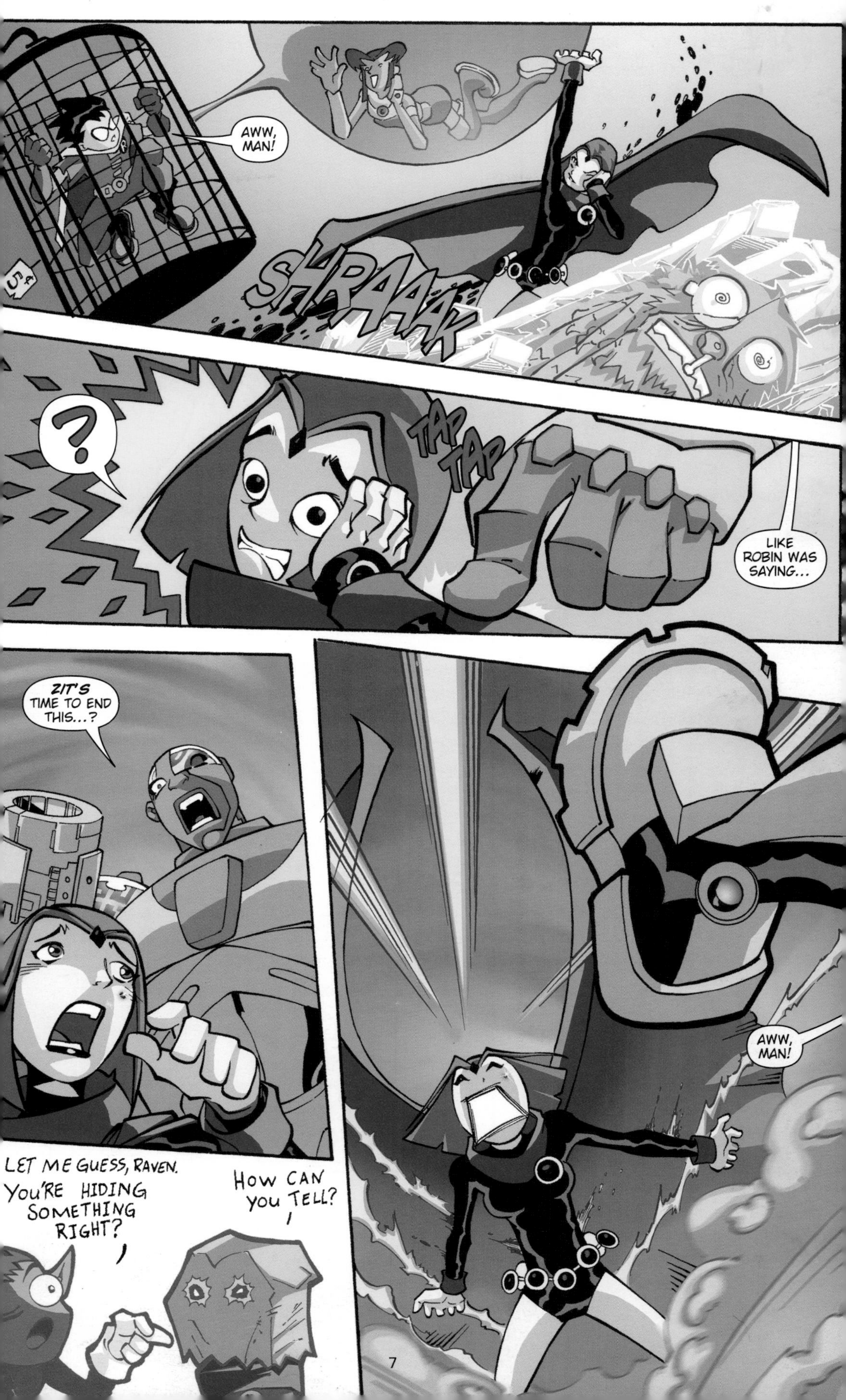

AWW, MAN!
SHRAAAK
?
TAP TAP
LIKE ROBIN WAS SAYING...
ZIT'S TIME TO END THIS...?
AWW, MAN!
LET ME GUESS, RAVEN. YOU'RE HIDING SOMETHING RIGHT?
HOW CAN YOU TELL?

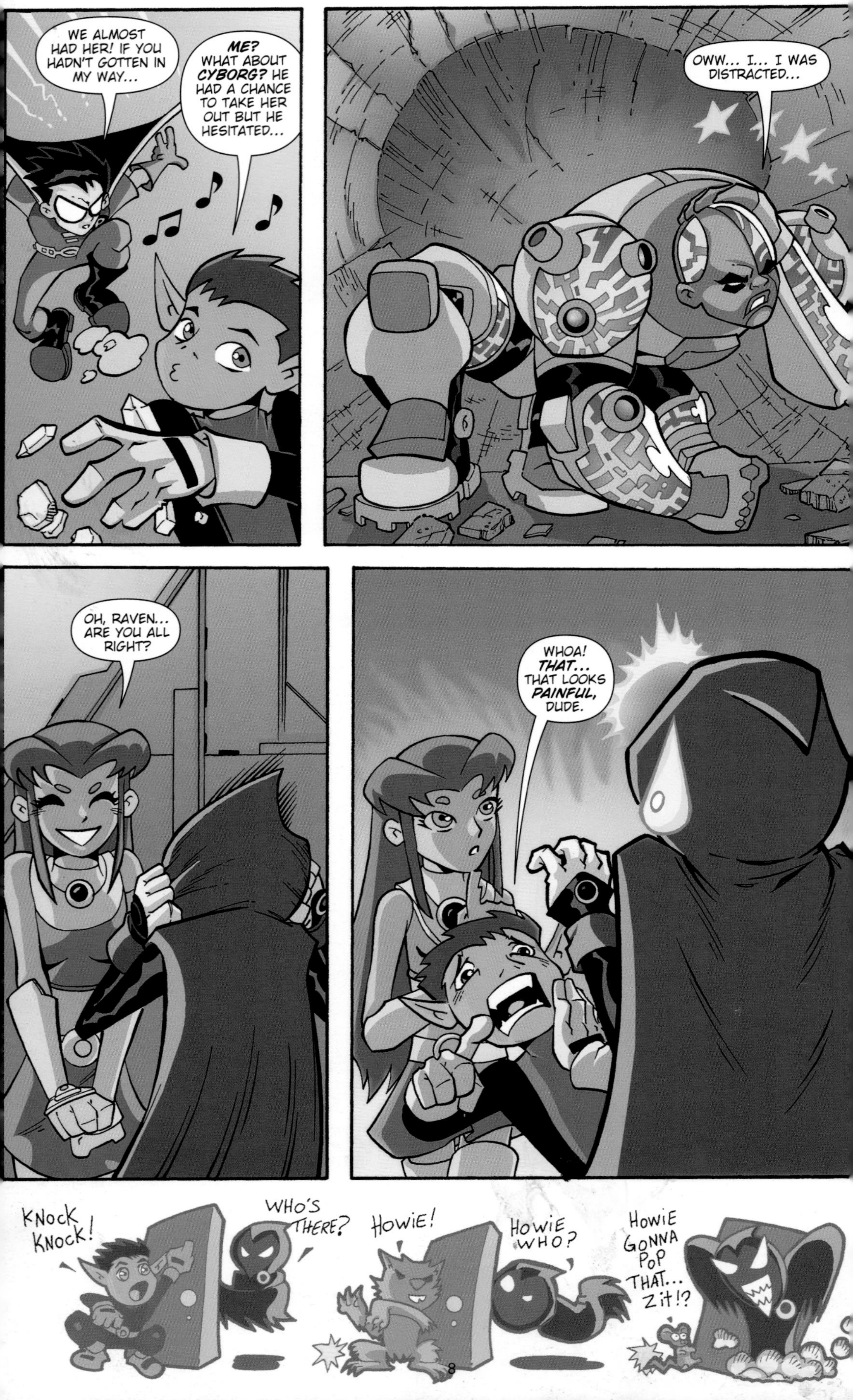
WE ALMOST HAD HER! IF YOU HADN'T GOTTEN IN MY WAY...
ME? WHAT ABOUT CYBORG? HE HAD A CHANCE TO TAKE HER OUT BUT HE HESITATED...
OWW... I... I WAS DISTRACTED...
OH, RAVEN... ARE YOU ALL RIGHT?
WHOA! THAT... THAT LOOKS PAINFUL, DUDE.
KNOCK KNOCK!
WHO'S THERE?
HOWIE!
HOWIE WHO?
HOWIE GONNA POP THAT... ZIT!?

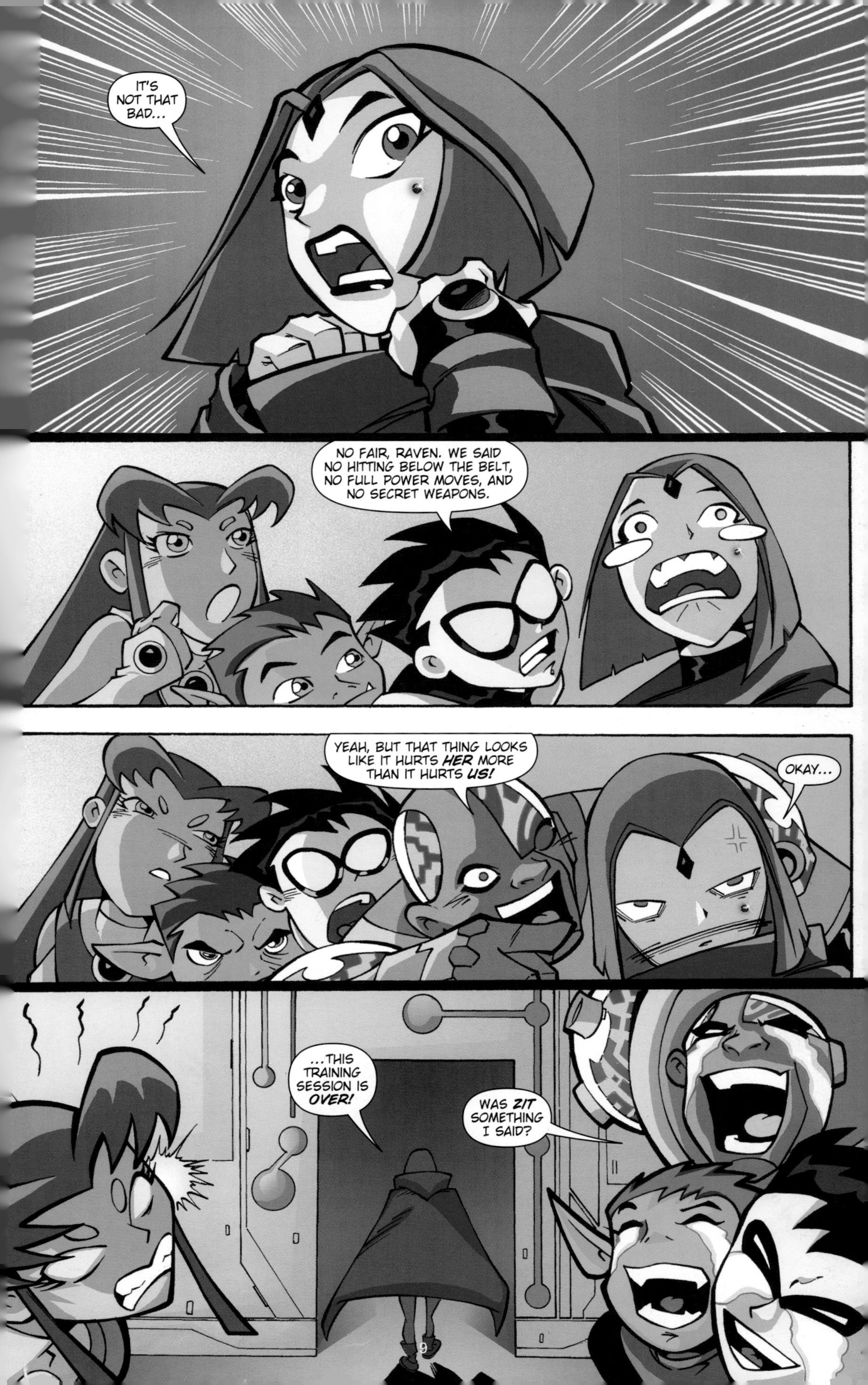
IT'S NOT THAT BAD...
NO FAIR, RAVEN. WE SAID NO HITTING BELOW THE BELT, NO FULL POWER MOVES, AND NO SECRET WEAPONS.
YEAH, BUT THAT THING LOOKS LIKE IT HURTS *HER* MORE THAN IT HURTS *US!*
OKAY...
...THIS TRAINING SESSION IS *OVER!*
WAS *ZIT* SOMETHING I SAID?

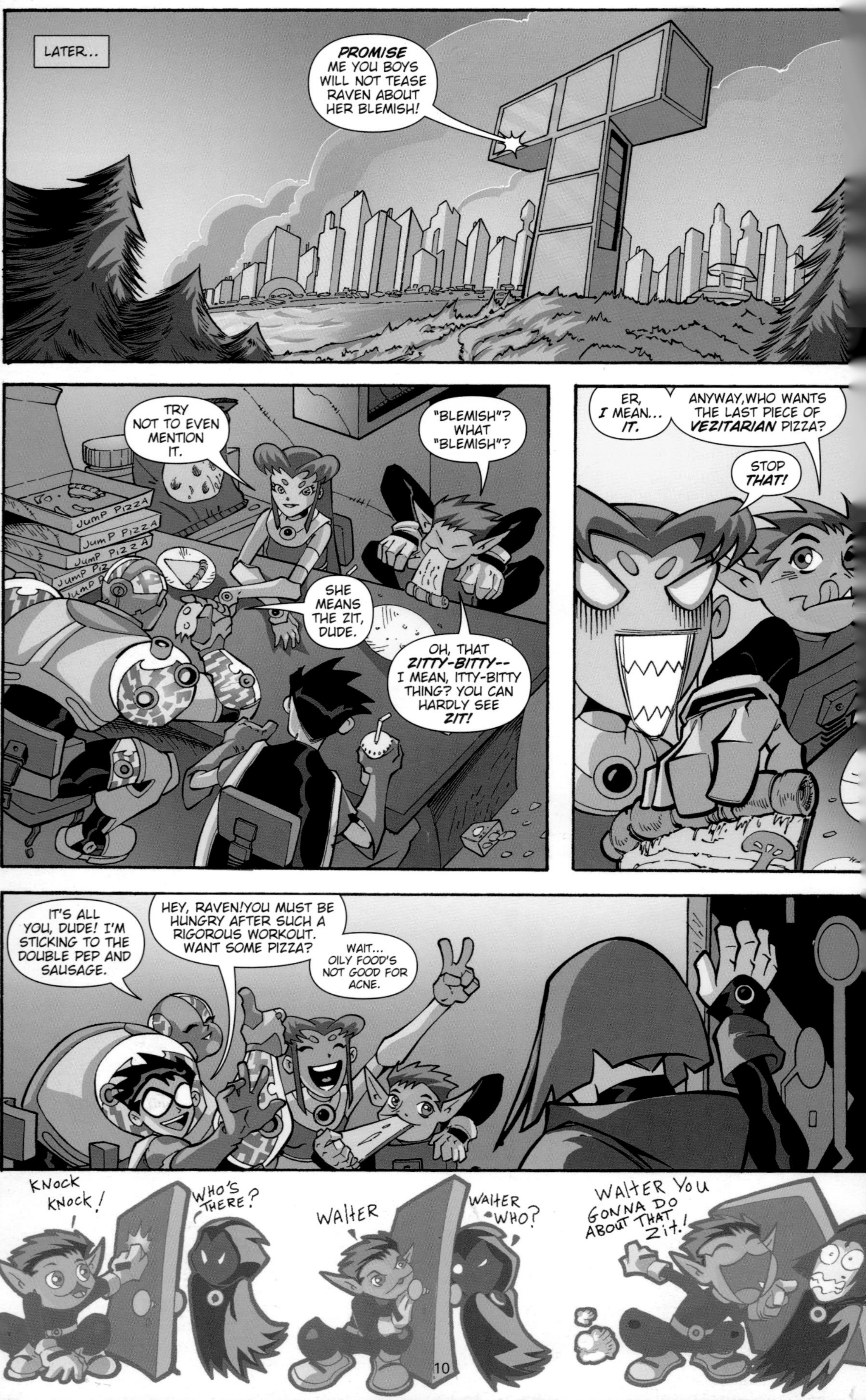
LATER...
PROMISE ME YOU BOYS WILL NOT TEASE RAVEN ABOUT HER BLEMISH!
TRY NOT TO EVEN MENTION IT.
"BLEMISH"? WHAT "BLEMISH"?
SHE MEANS THE ZIT, DUDE.
OH, THAT ZITTY-BITTY-- I MEAN, ITTY-BITTY THING? YOU CAN HARDLY SEE ZIT!
JUMP PIZZA
ER, I MEAN... IT.
ANYWAY, WHO WANTS THE LAST PIECE OF VEZITARIAN PIZZA?
STOP THAT!
IT'S ALL YOU, DUDE! I'M STICKING TO THE DOUBLE PEP AND SAUSAGE.
HEY, RAVEN! YOU MUST BE HUNGRY AFTER SUCH A RIGOROUS WORKOUT. WANT SOME PIZZA?
WAIT... OILY FOOD'S NOT GOOD FOR ACNE.
KNOCK KNOCK!
WHO'S THERE?
WALTER
WALTER WHO?
WALTER YOU GONNA DO ABOUT THAT ZIT!

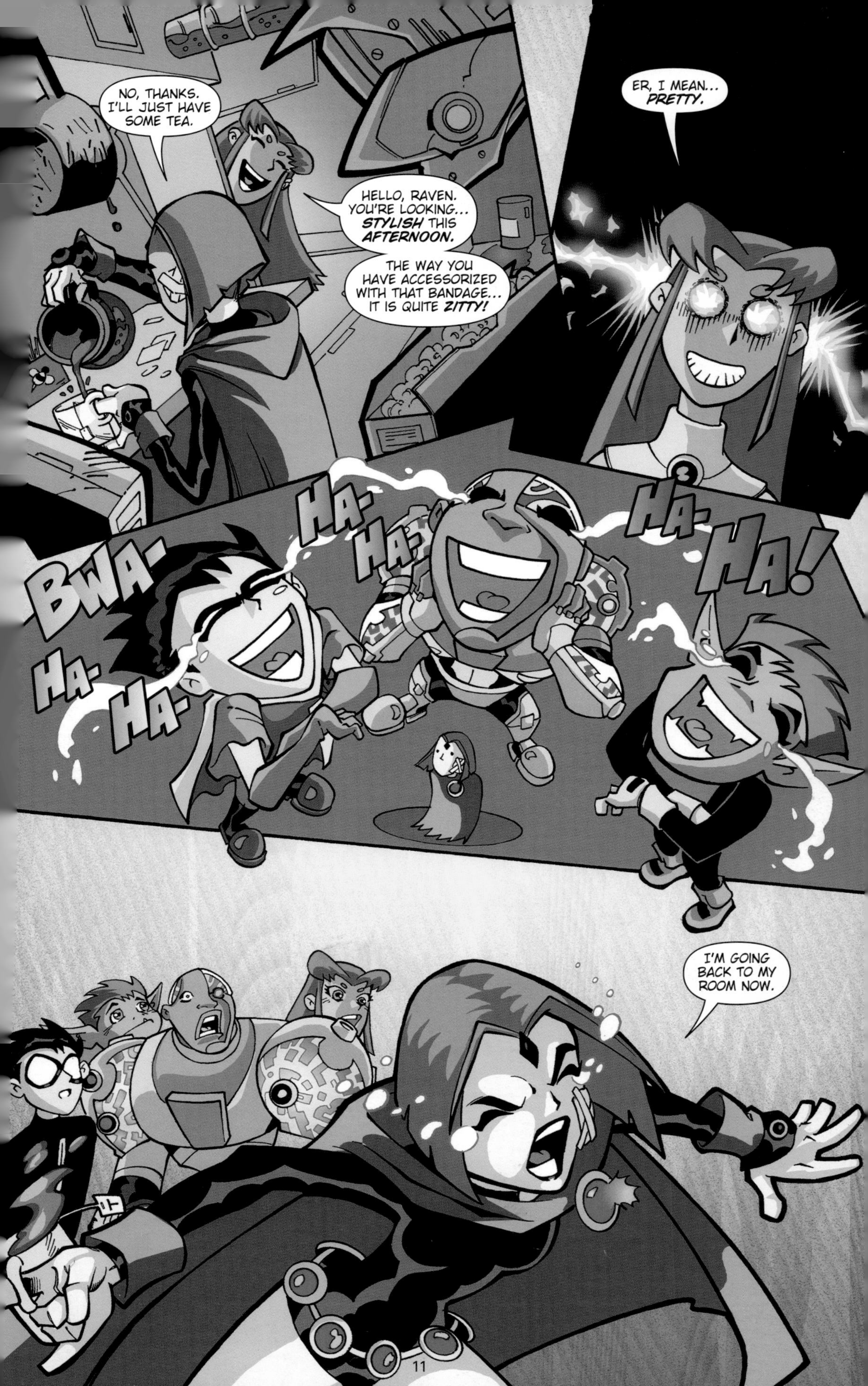

NO, THANKS. I'LL JUST HAVE SOME TEA.
HELLO, RAVEN. YOU'RE LOOKING... STYLISH THIS AFTERNOON.
THE WAY YOU HAVE ACCESSORIZED WITH THAT BANDAGE... IT IS QUITE ZITTY!
ER, I MEAN... PRETTY.
BWA-HA-HA-
HA-HA-
HA-HA!
I'M GOING BACK TO MY ROOM NOW.

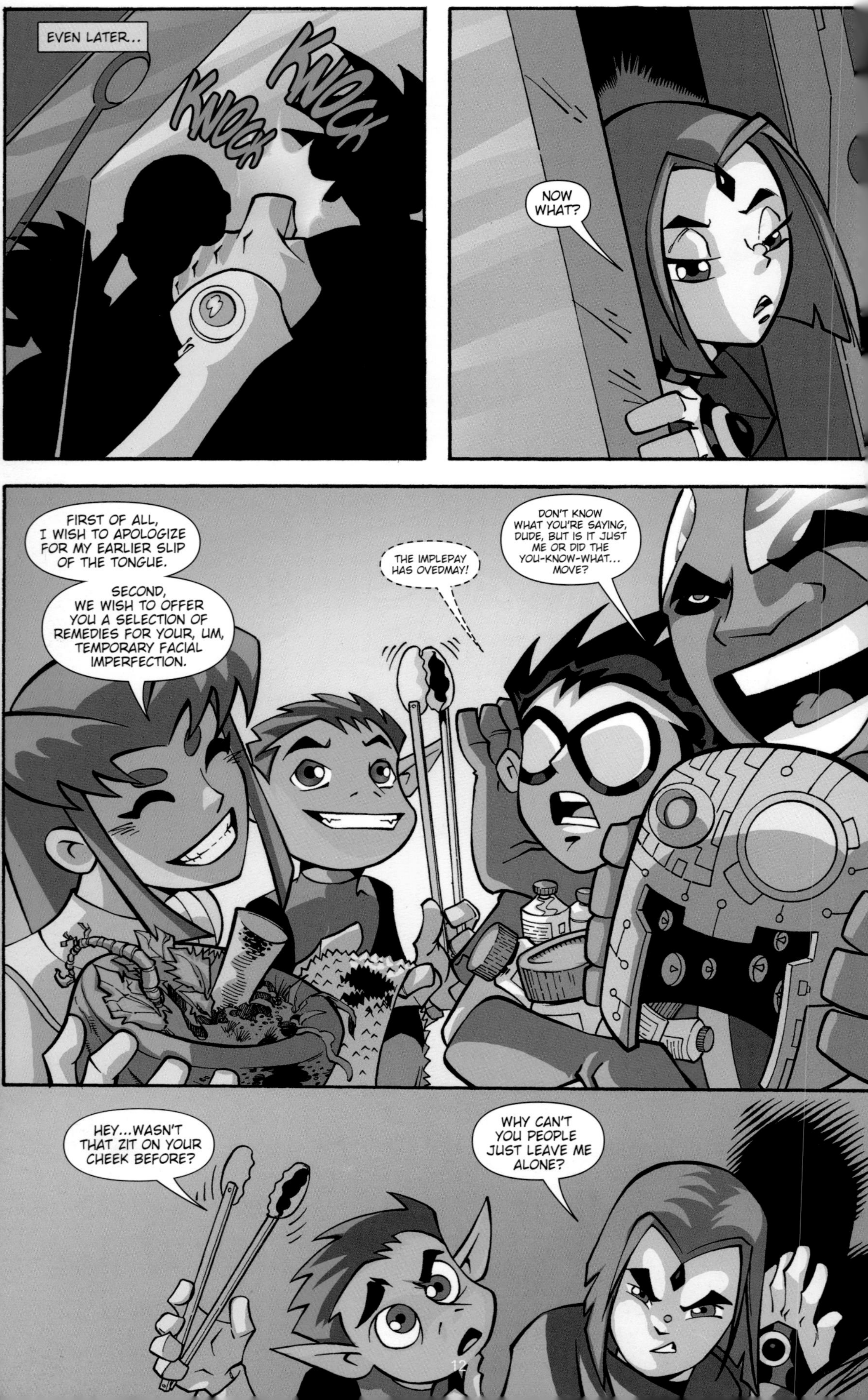
EVEN LATER...
KNOCK
KNOCK
NOW WHAT?
FIRST OF ALL, I WISH TO APOLOGIZE FOR MY EARLIER SLIP OF THE TONGUE.
SECOND, WE WISH TO OFFER YOU A SELECTION OF REMEDIES FOR YOUR, UM, TEMPORARY FACIAL IMPERFECTION.
THE IMPLEPAY HAS OVEDMAY!
DON'T KNOW WHAT YOU'RE SAYING, DUDE, BUT IS IT JUST ME OR DID THE YOU-KNOW-WHAT... MOVE?
HEY...WASN'T THAT ZIT ON YOUR CHEEK BEFORE?
WHY CAN'T YOU PEOPLE JUST LEAVE ME ALONE?

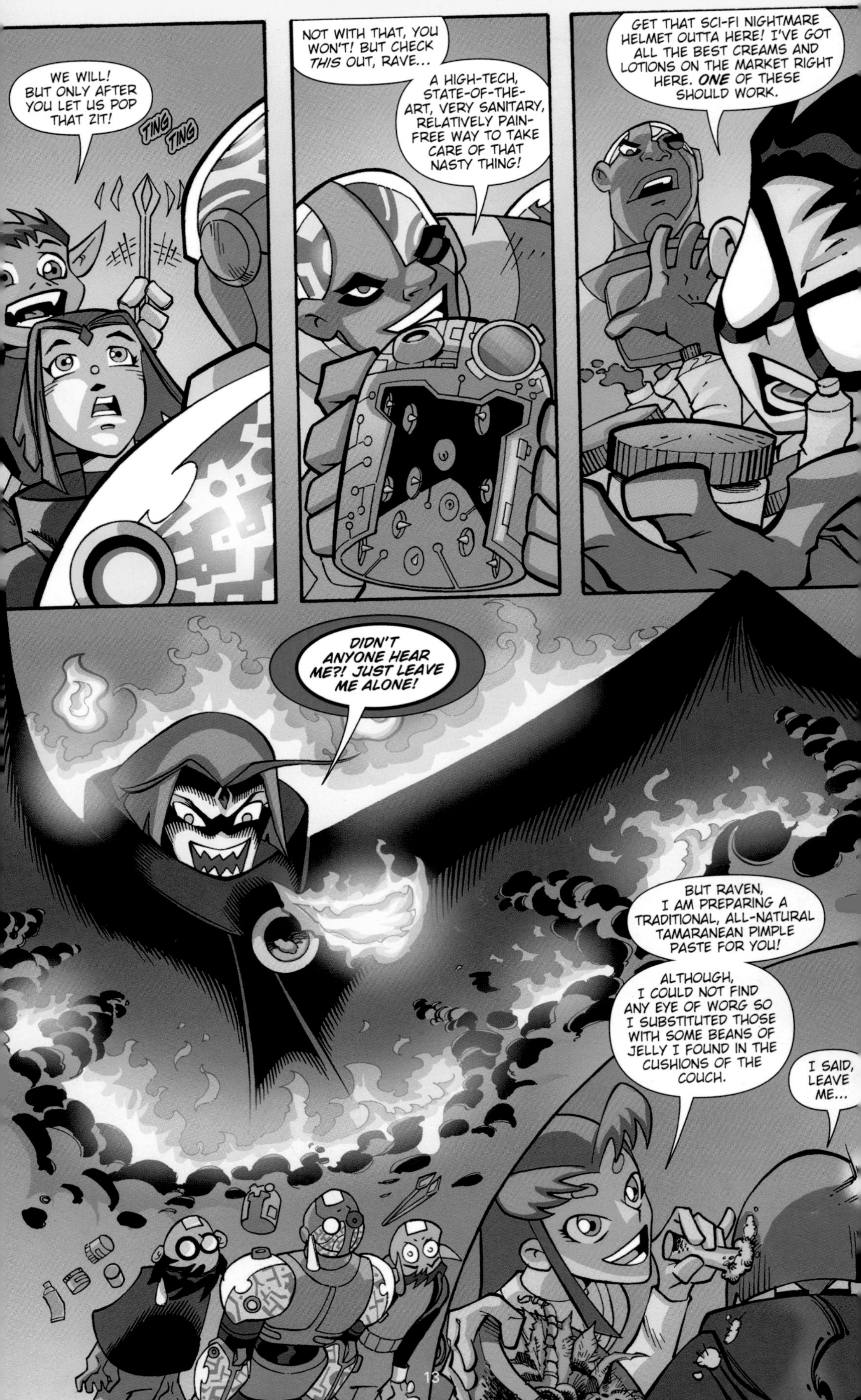
WE WILL! BUT ONLY AFTER YOU LET US POP THAT ZIT!
TING TING
NOT WITH THAT, YOU WON'T! BUT CHECK *THIS* OUT, RAVE...
A HIGH-TECH, STATE-OF-THE-ART, VERY SANITARY, RELATIVELY PAIN-FREE WAY TO TAKE CARE OF THAT NASTY THING!
GET THAT SCI-FI NIGHTMARE HELMET OUTTA HERE! I'VE GOT ALL THE BEST CREAMS AND LOTIONS ON THE MARKET RIGHT HERE. ***ONE*** OF THESE SHOULD WORK.
DIDN'T ANYONE HEAR ME?! JUST LEAVE ME ALONE!
BUT RAVEN, I AM PREPARING A TRADITIONAL, ALL-NATURAL TAMARANEAN PIMPLE PASTE FOR YOU!
ALTHOUGH, I COULD NOT FIND ANY EYE OF WORG SO I SUBSTITUTED THOSE WITH SOME BEANS OF JELLY I FOUND IN THE CUSHIONS OF THE COUCH.
I SAID, LEAVE ME...

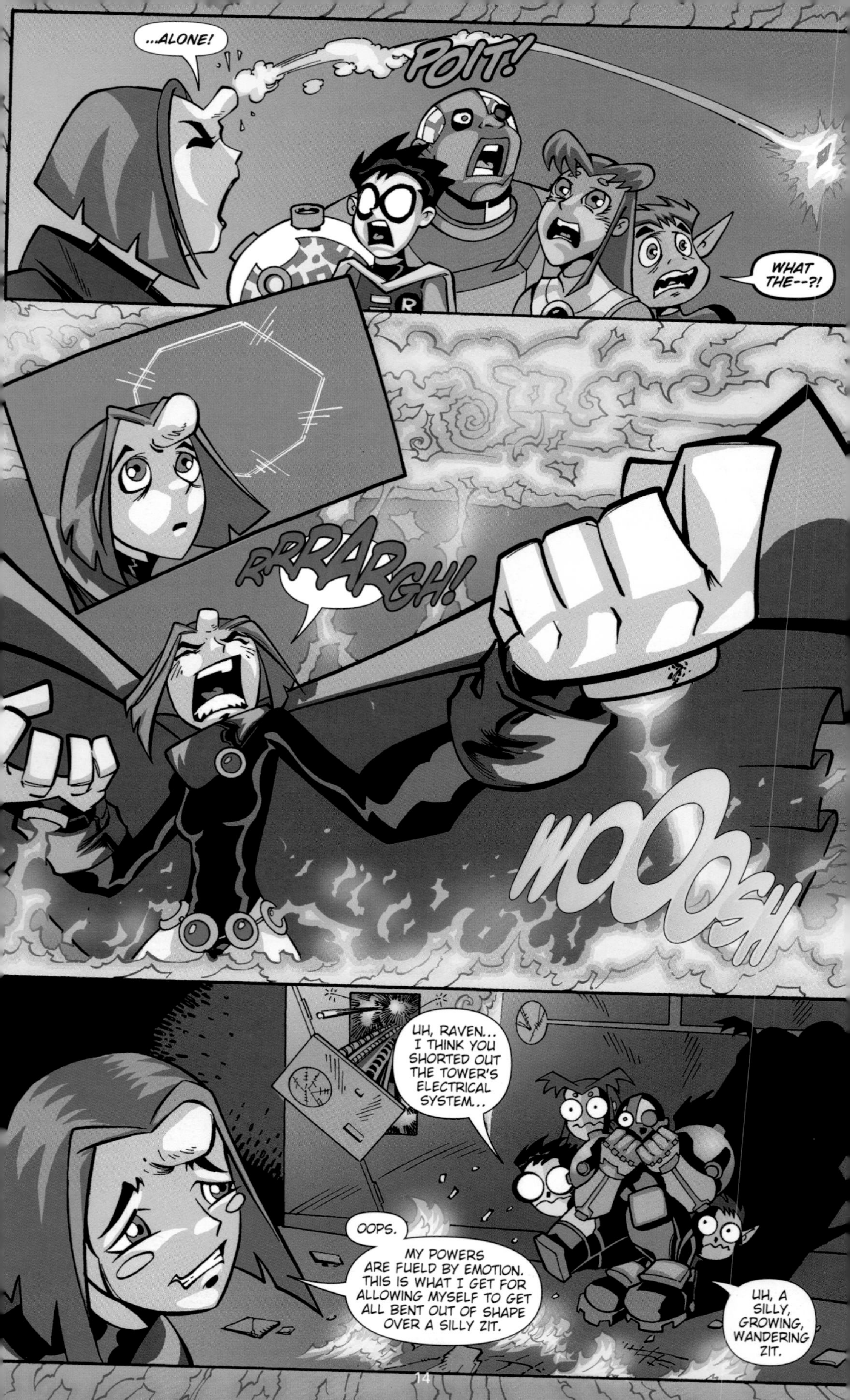
...ALONE!
POIT!
WHAT THE--?!
RRRARGH!
WOOOSH
UH, RAVEN... I THINK YOU SHORTED OUT THE TOWER'S ELECTRICAL SYSTEM...
OOPS.
MY POWERS ARE FUELD BY EMOTION. THIS IS WHAT I GET FOR ALLOWING MYSELF TO GET ALL BENT OUT OF SHAPE OVER A SILLY ZIT.
UH, A SILLY, GROWING, WANDERING ZIT.

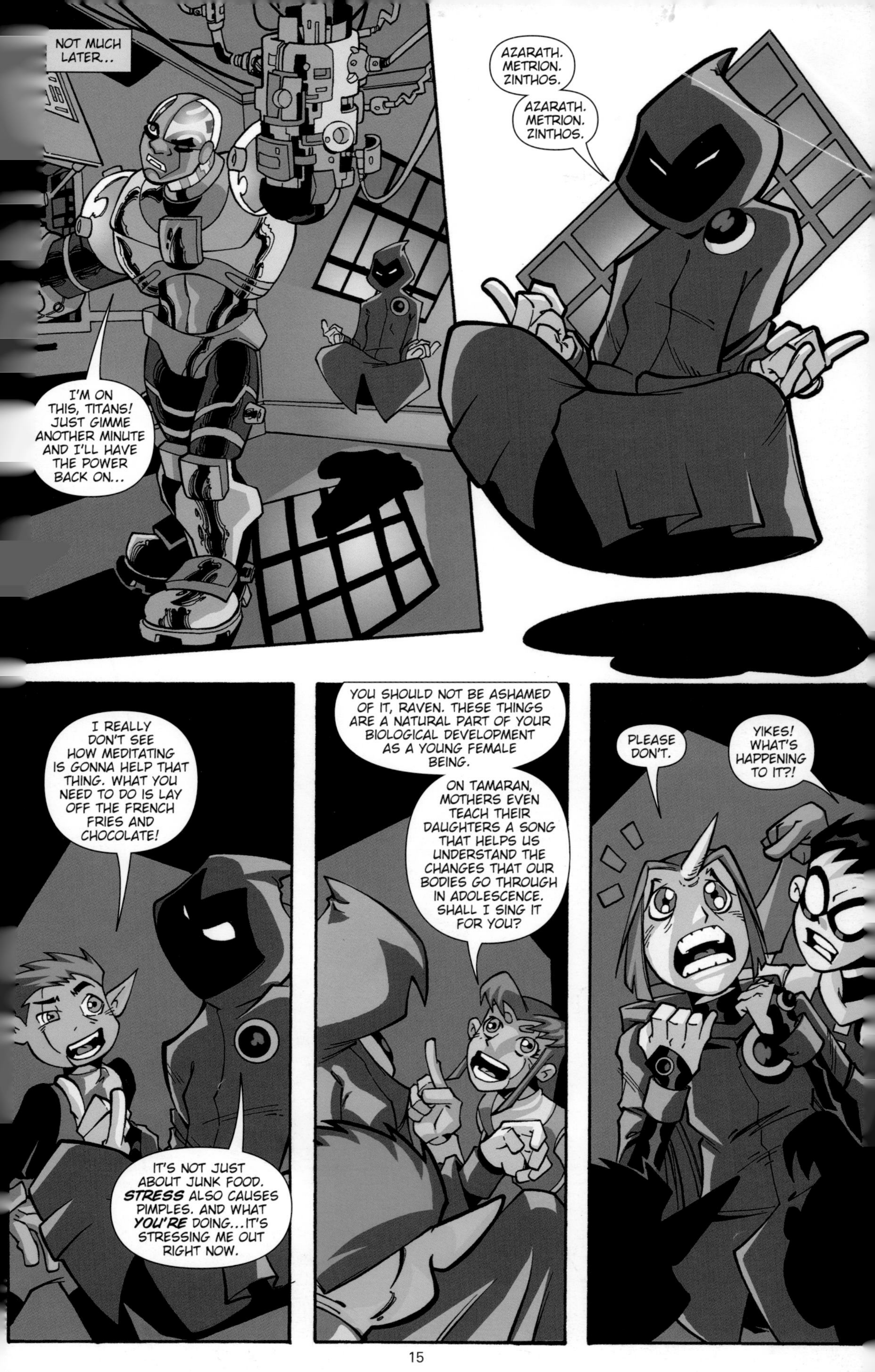
NOT MUCH LATER...
I'M ON THIS, TITANS! JUST GIMME ANOTHER MINUTE AND I'LL HAVE THE POWER BACK ON...
AZARATH. METRION. ZINTHOS.
AZARATH. METRION. ZINTHOS.
I REALLY DON'T SEE HOW MEDITATING IS GONNA HELP THAT THING. WHAT YOU NEED TO DO IS LAY OFF THE FRENCH FRIES AND CHOCOLATE!
IT'S NOT JUST ABOUT JUNK FOOD. STRESS ALSO CAUSES PIMPLES. AND WHAT YOU'RE DOING...IT'S STRESSING ME OUT RIGHT NOW.
YOU SHOULD NOT BE ASHAMED OF IT, RAVEN. THESE THINGS ARE A NATURAL PART OF YOUR BIOLOGICAL DEVELOPMENT AS A YOUNG FEMALE BEING.
ON TAMARAN, MOTHERS EVEN TEACH THEIR DAUGHTERS A SONG THAT HELPS US UNDERSTAND THE CHANGES THAT OUR BODIES GO THROUGH IN ADOLESCENCE. SHALL I SING IT FOR YOU?
PLEASE DON'T.
YIKES! WHAT'S HAPPENING TO IT?!

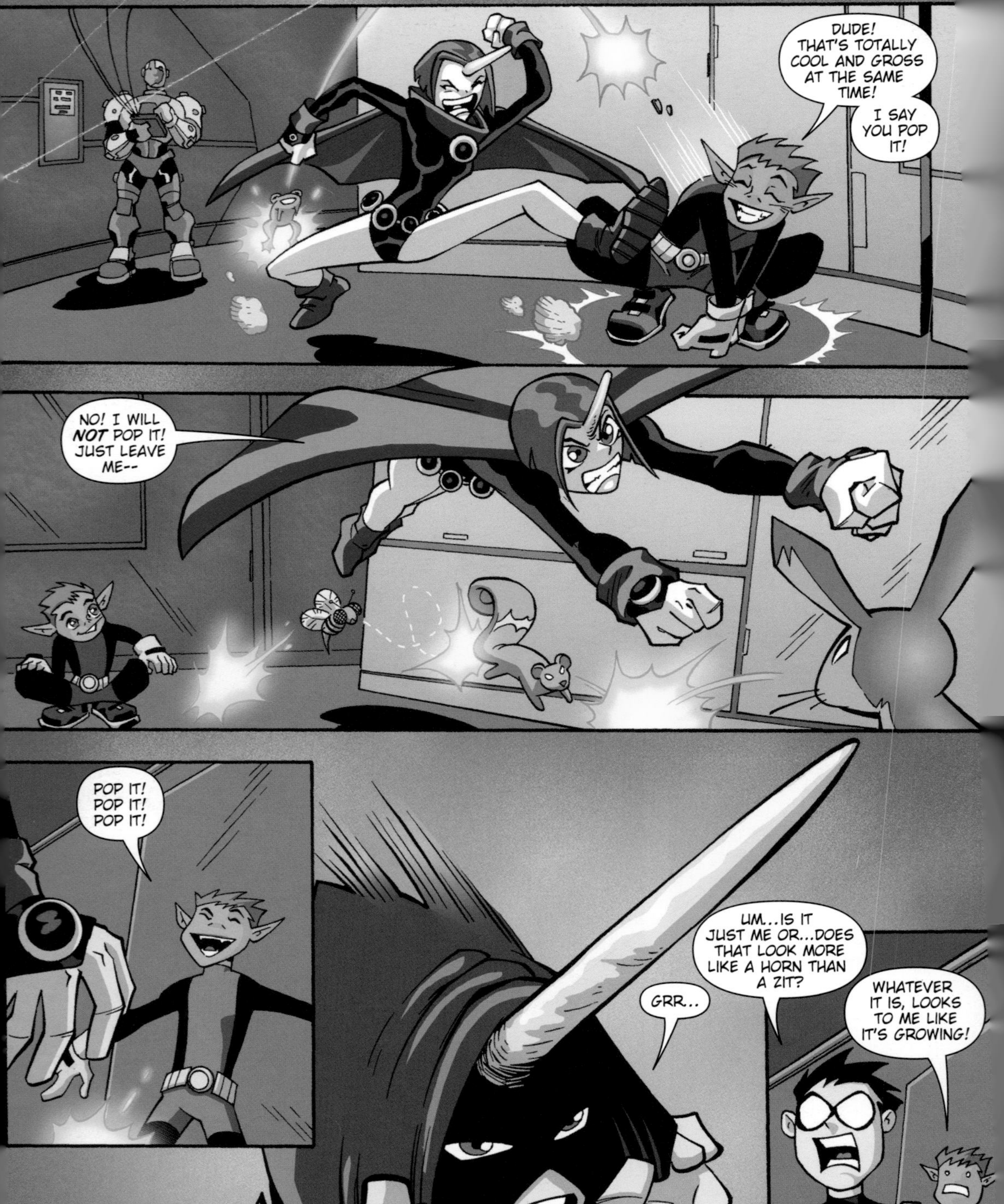
DUDE! THAT'S TOTALLY COOL AND GROSS AT THE SAME TIME!
I SAY YOU POP IT!
NO! I WILL *NOT* POP IT! JUST LEAVE ME--
POP IT! POP IT! POP IT!
UM...IS IT JUST ME OR...DOES THAT LOOK MORE LIKE A HORN THAN A ZIT?
GRR...
WHATEVER IT IS, LOOKS TO ME LIKE IT'S GROWING!
R

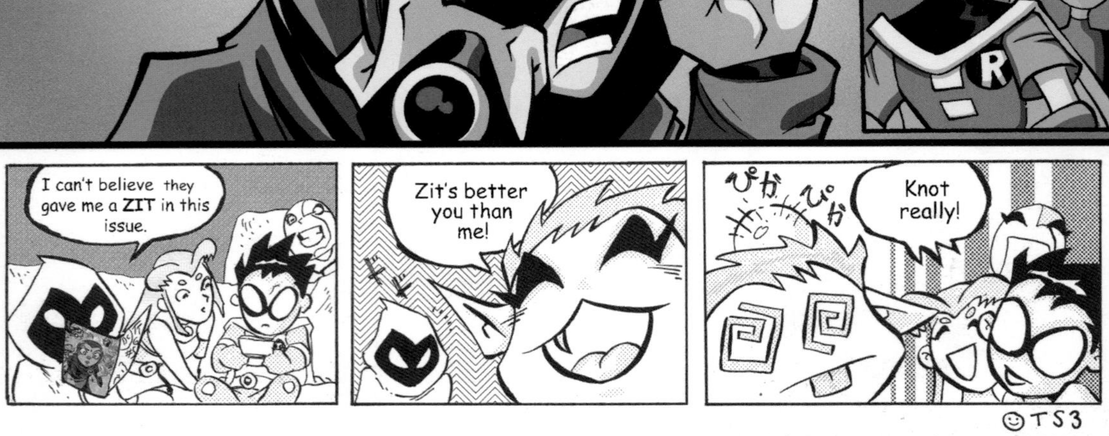
I can't believe they gave me a **ZIT** in this issue.
Zit's better you than me!
ぴか ぴか
Knot really!

©TS3

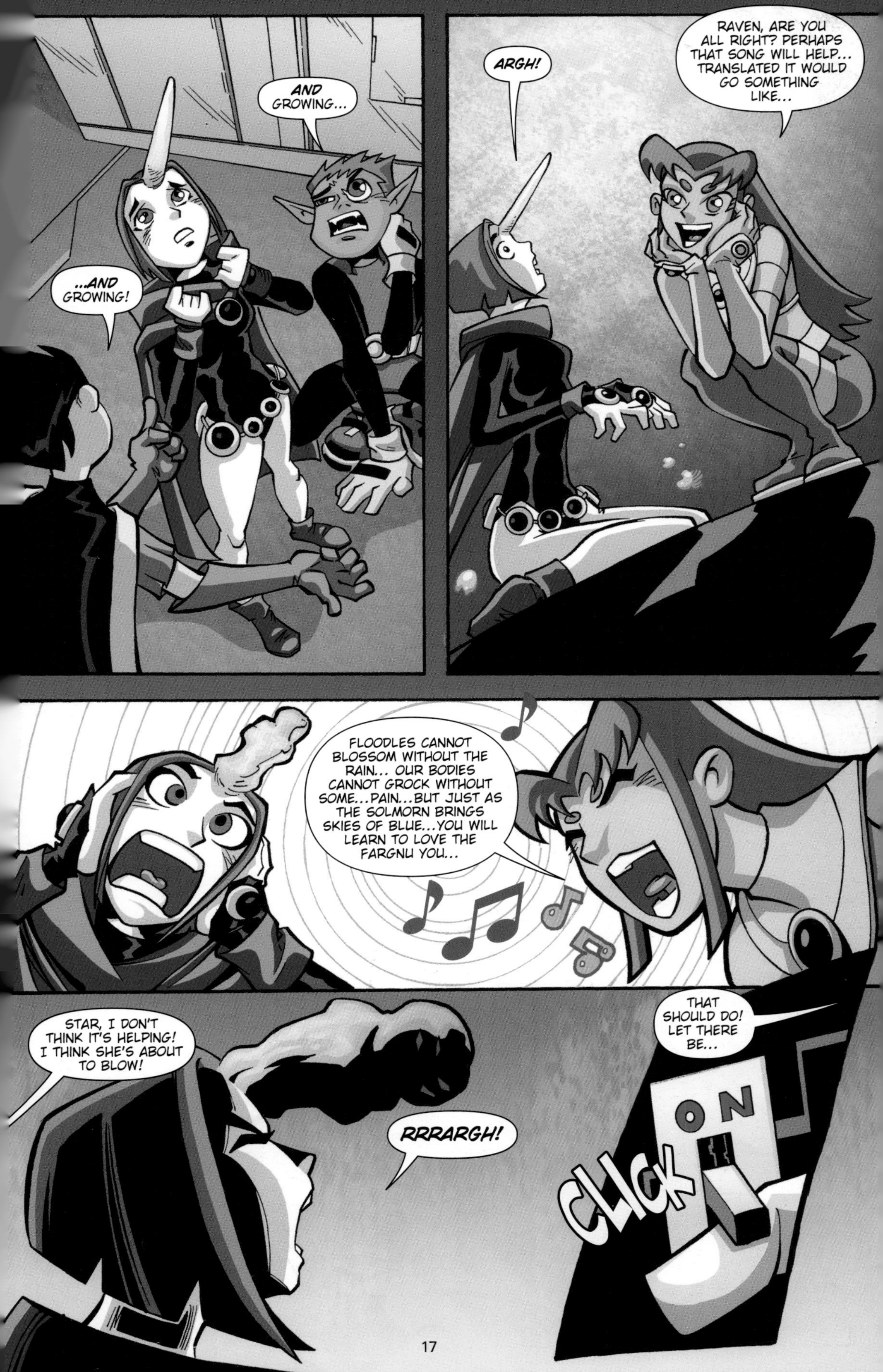
AND GROWING...
...AND GROWING!
ARGH!
RAVEN, ARE YOU ALL RIGHT? PERHAPS THAT SONG WILL HELP... TRANSLATED IT WOULD GO SOMETHING LIKE...
FLOODLES CANNOT BLOSSOM WITHOUT THE RAIN... OUR BODIES CANNOT GROCK WITHOUT SOME...PAIN...BUT JUST AS THE SOLMORN BRINGS SKIES OF BLUE...YOU WILL LEARN TO LOVE THE FARGNU YOU...
STAR, I DON'T THINK IT'S HELPING! I THINK SHE'S ABOUT TO BLOW!
RRRARGH!
THAT SHOULD DO! LET THERE BE...
ON
CLICK

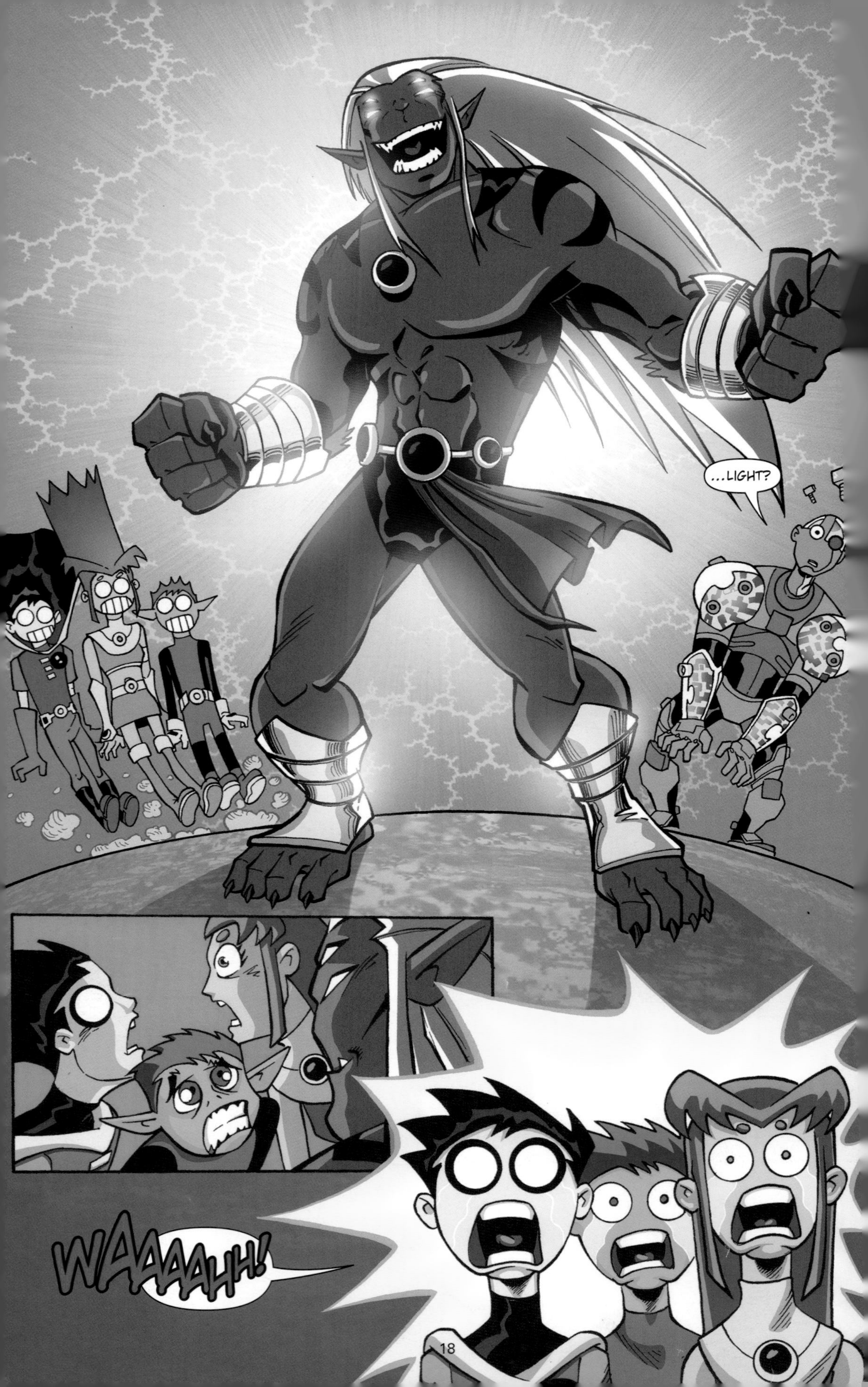
...LIGHT?
WAAAAHH!

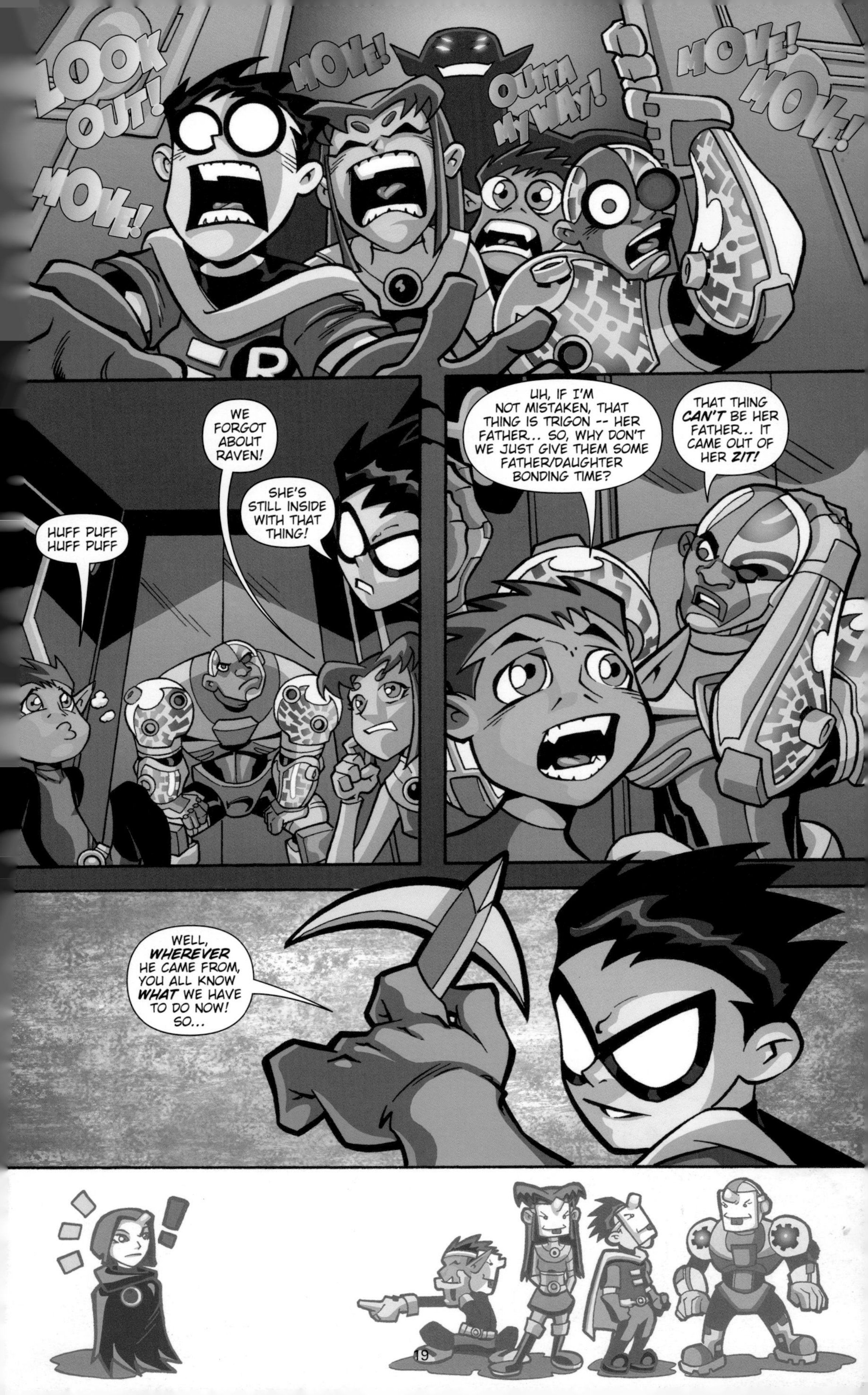
LOOK OUT!
MOVE!
MOVE!
OUTTA MY WAY!
MOVE! MOVE! MOVE!
HUFF PUFF HUFF PUFF
WE FORGOT ABOUT RAVEN!
SHE'S STILL INSIDE WITH THAT THING!
UH, IF I'M NOT MISTAKEN, THAT THING IS TRIGON -- HER FATHER.. SO, WHY DON'T WE JUST GIVE THEM SOME FATHER/DAUGHTER BONDING TIME?
THAT THING CAN'T BE HER FATHER... IT CAME OUT OF HER ZIT!
WELL, WHEREVER HE CAME FROM, YOU ALL KNOW WHAT WE HAVE TO DO NOW! SO...

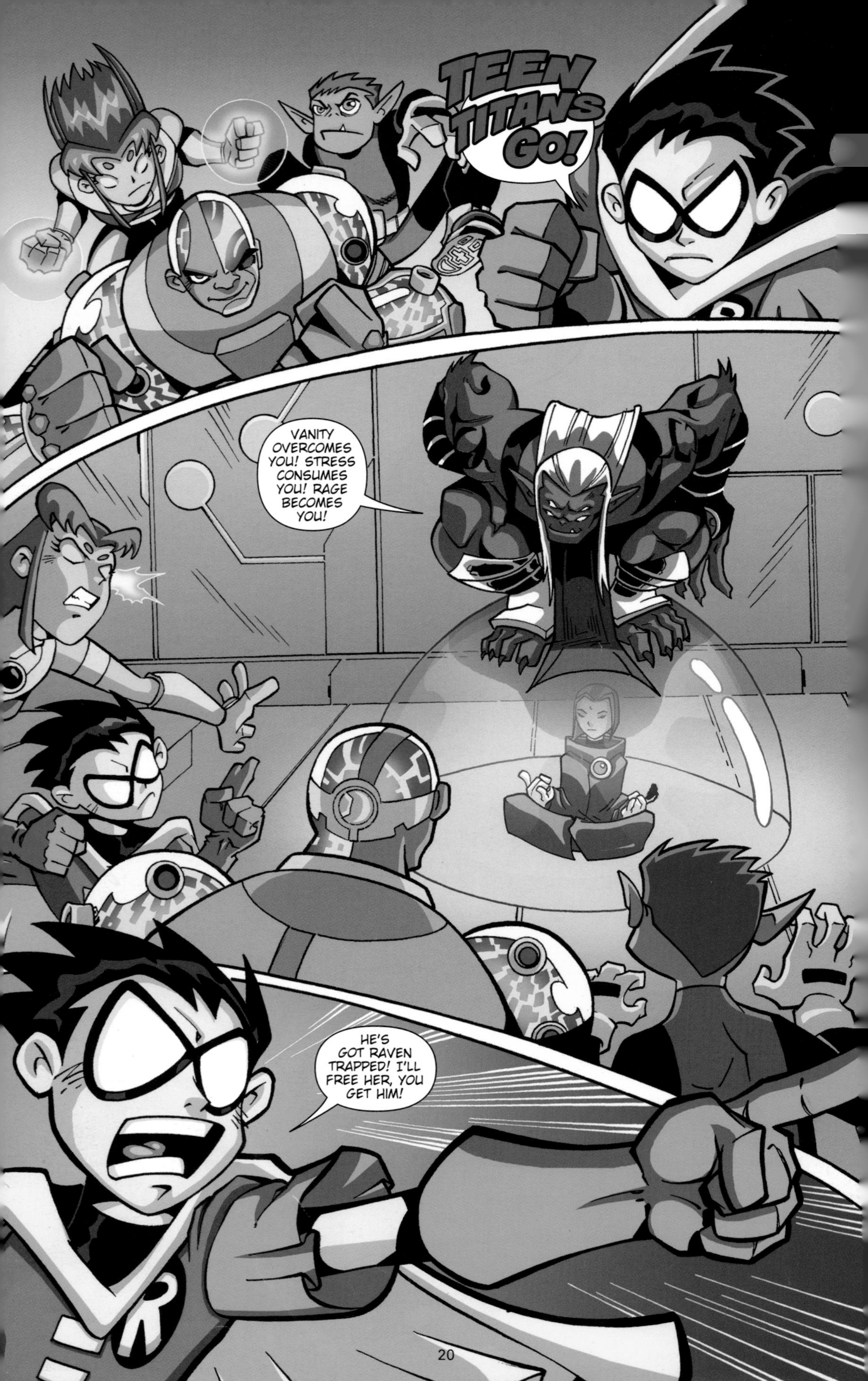
TEEN TITANS GO!
VANITY OVERCOMES YOU! STRESS CONSUMES YOU! RAGE BECOMES YOU!
HE'S GOT RAVEN TRAPPED! I'LL FREE HER, YOU GET HIM!

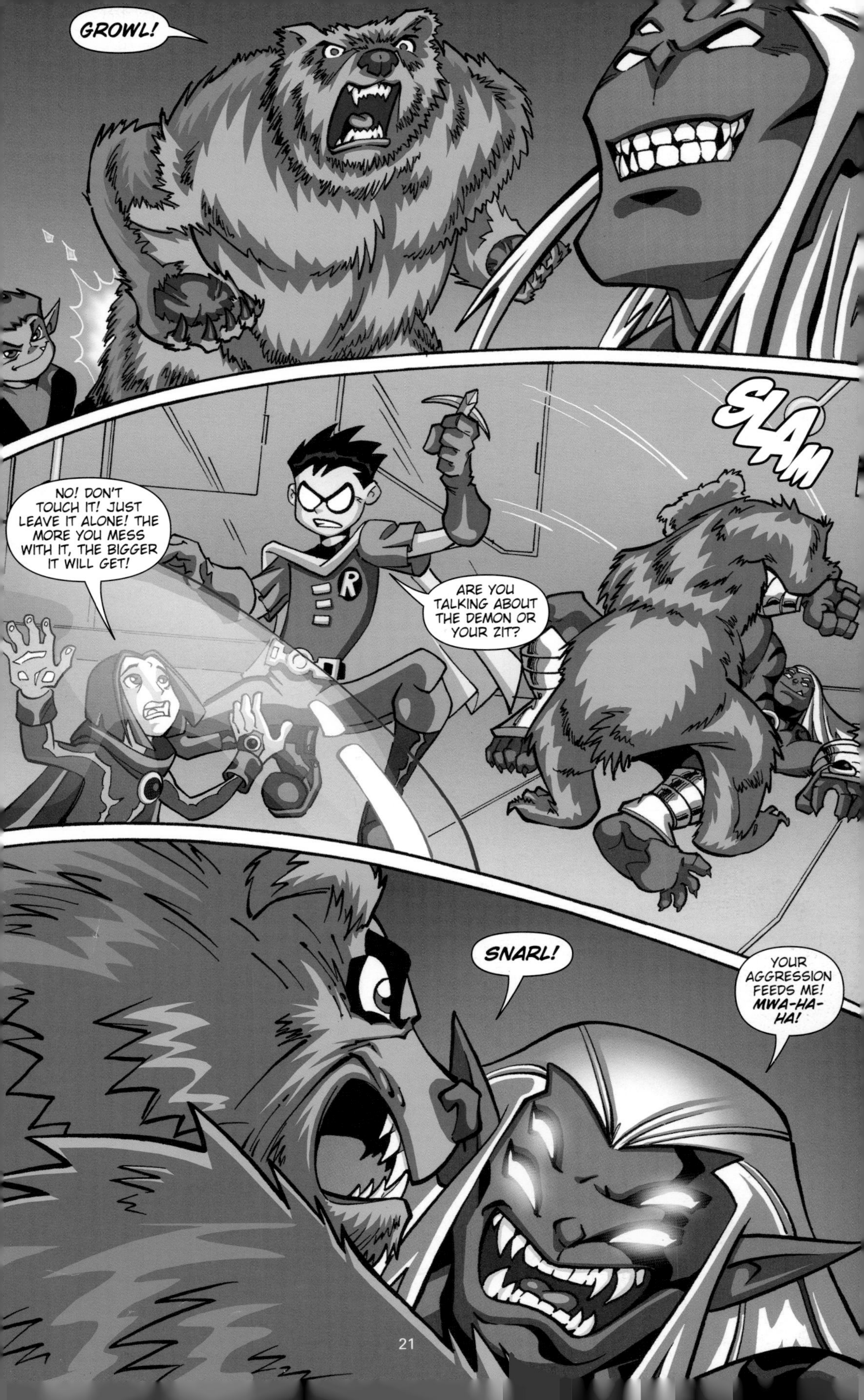
GROWL!
SLAM
NO! DON'T TOUCH IT! JUST LEAVE IT ALONE! THE MORE YOU MESS WITH IT, THE BIGGER IT WILL GET!
ARE YOU TALKING ABOUT THE DEMON OR YOUR ZIT?
SNARL!
YOUR AGGRESSION FEEDS ME! MWA-HA-HA!

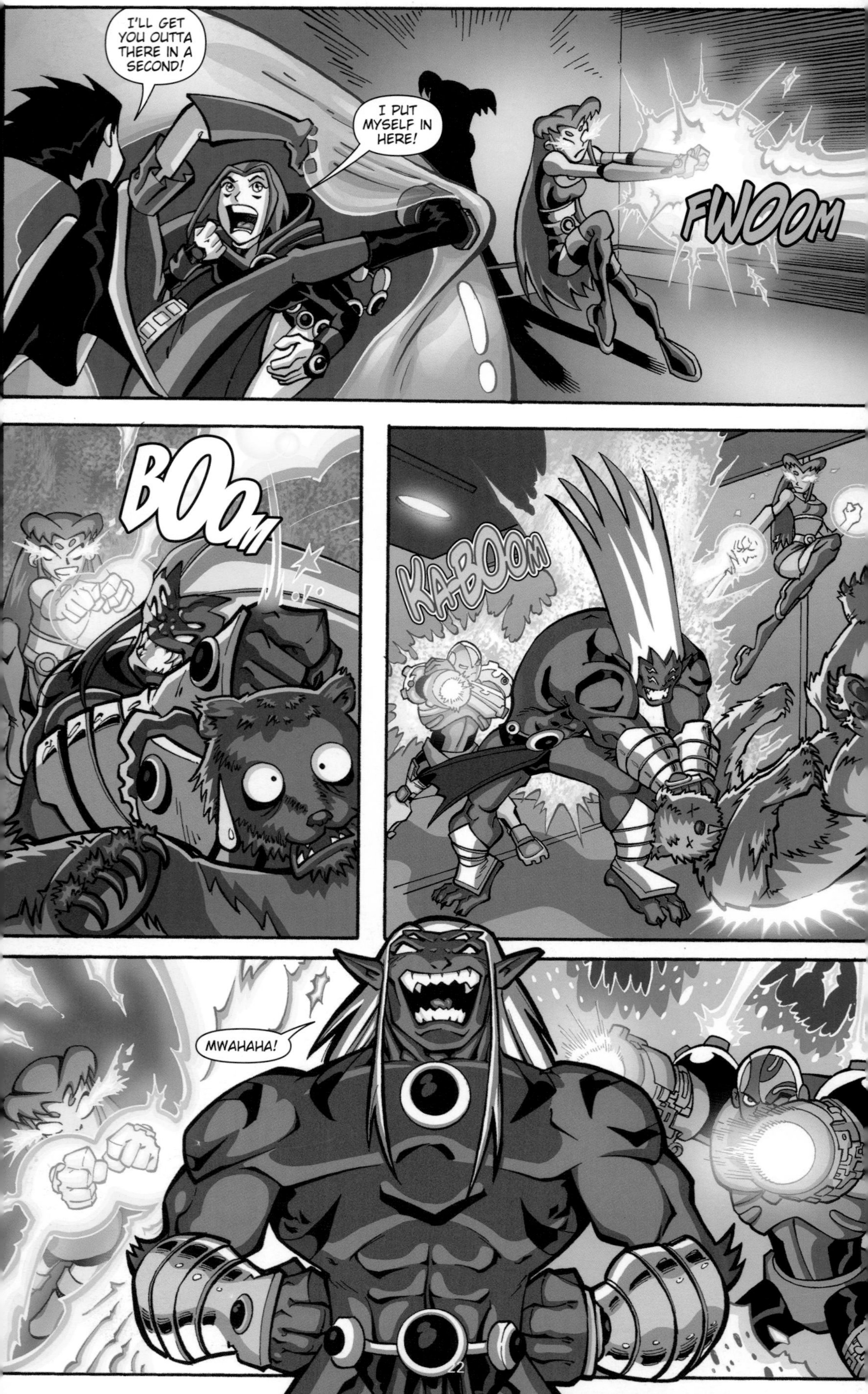
I'LL GET YOU OUTTA THERE IN A SECOND!
I PUT MYSELF IN HERE!
FWOOM
BOOM
KA-BOOM
MWAHAHA!

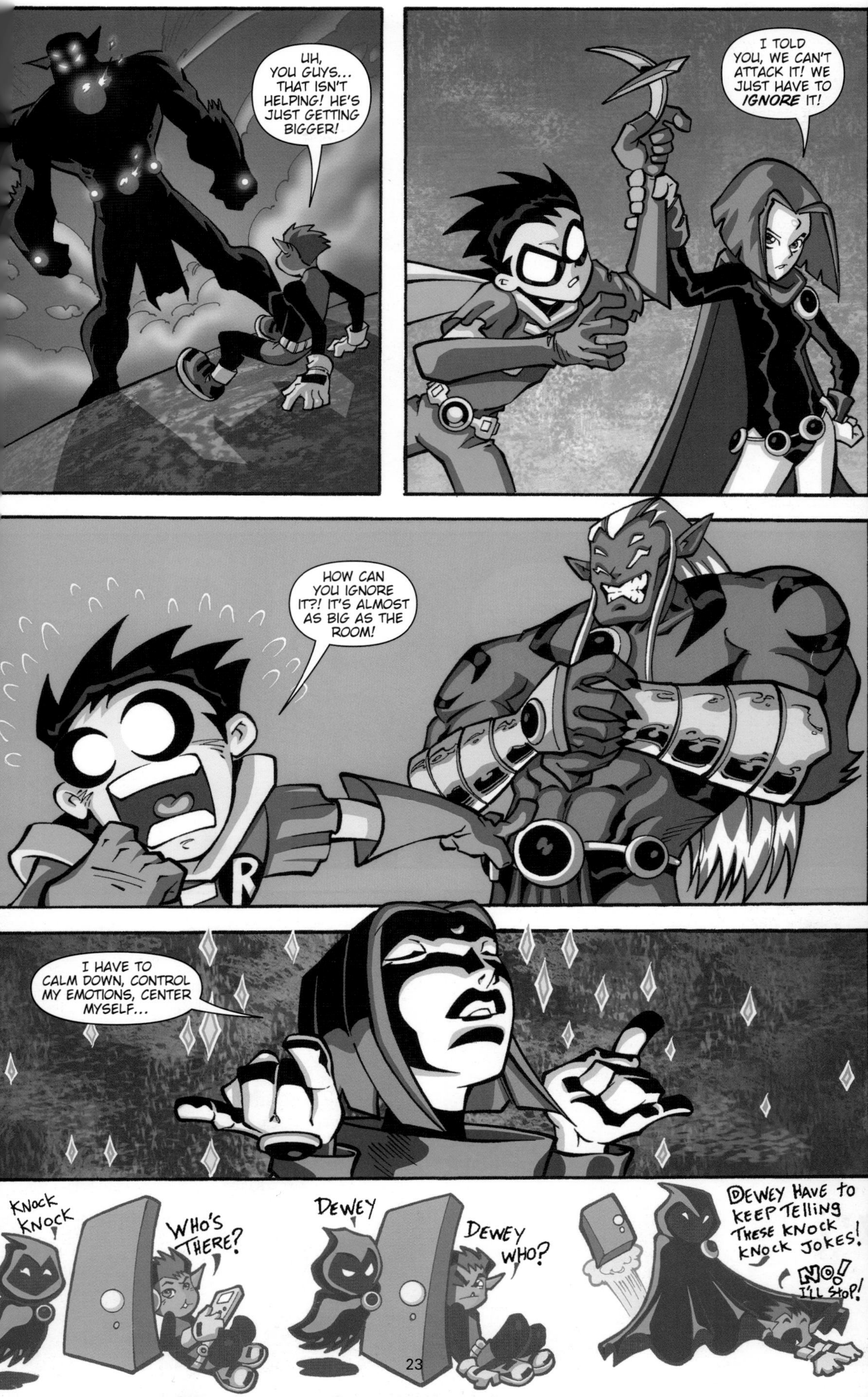
UH, YOU GUYS... THAT ISN'T HELPING! HE'S JUST GETTING BIGGER!
I TOLD YOU, WE CAN'T ATTACK IT! WE JUST HAVE TO IGNORE IT!
HOW CAN YOU IGNORE IT?! IT'S ALMOST AS BIG AS THE ROOM!
I HAVE TO CALM DOWN, CONTROL MY EMOTIONS, CENTER MYSELF...
KNOCK KNOCK
WHO'S THERE?
DEWEY
DEWEY WHO?
DEWEY HAVE TO KEEP TELLING THESE KNOCK KNOCK JOKES!
NO! I'LL STOP!

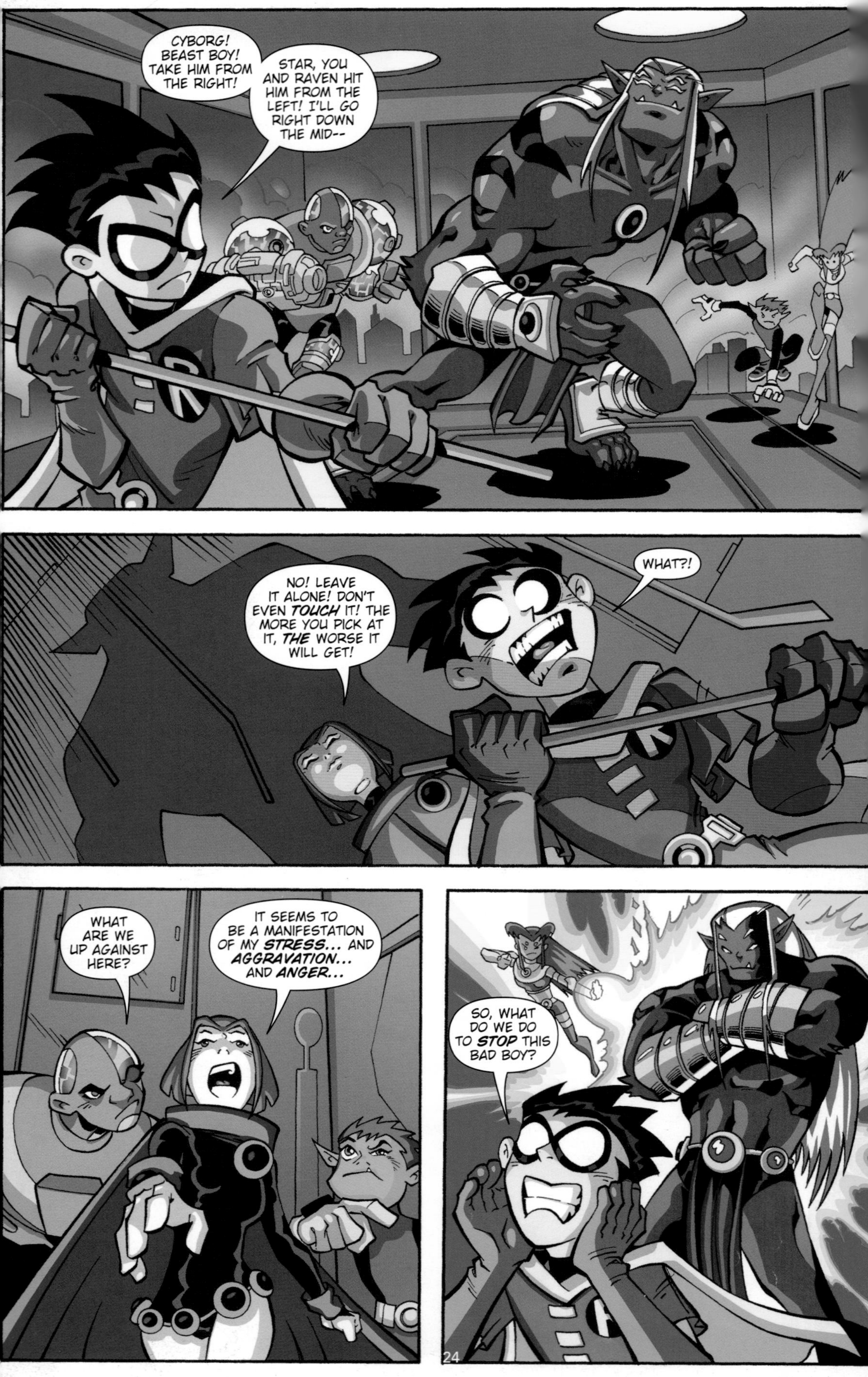
CYBORG! BEAST BOY! TAKE HIM FROM THE RIGHT!
STAR, YOU AND RAVEN HIT HIM FROM THE LEFT! I'LL GO RIGHT DOWN THE MID--
WHAT?!
NO! LEAVE IT ALONE! DON'T EVEN TOUCH IT! THE MORE YOU PICK AT IT, THE WORSE IT WILL GET!
WHAT ARE WE UP AGAINST HERE?
IT SEEMS TO BE A MANIFESTATION OF MY STRESS... AND AGGRAVATION... AND ANGER...
SO, WHAT DO WE DO TO STOP THIS BAD BOY?

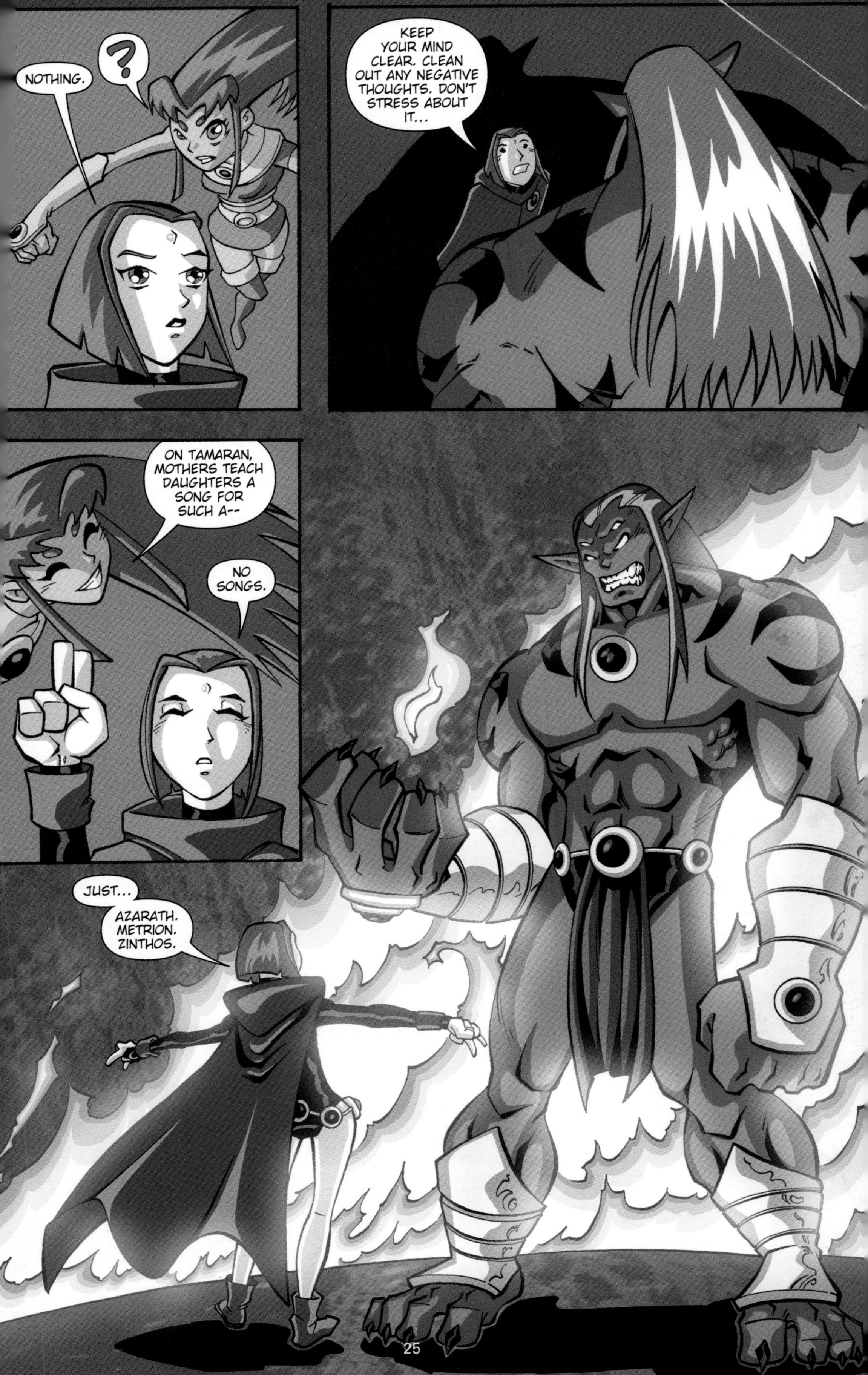
NOTHING.
?
KEEP YOUR MIND CLEAR. CLEAN OUT ANY NEGATIVE THOUGHTS. DON'T STRESS ABOUT IT...
ON TAMARAN, MOTHERS TEACH DAUGHTERS A SONG FOR SUCH A--
NO SONGS.
JUST...
AZARATH. METRION. ZINTHOS.

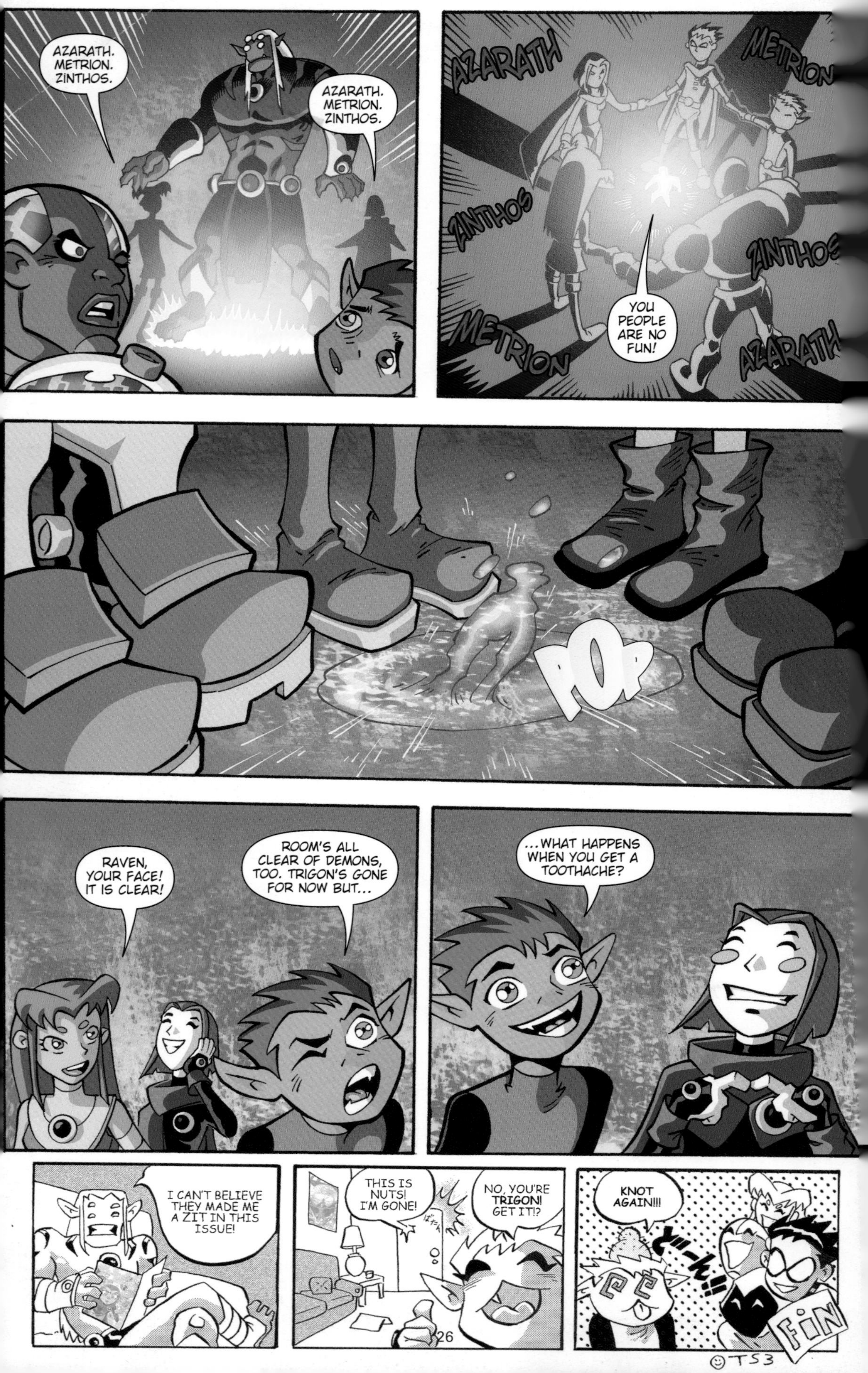
AZARATH. METRION. ZINTHOS.
AZARATH. METRION. ZINTHOS.
AZARATH
METRION
ZINTHOS
ZINTHOS
YOU PEOPLE ARE NO FUN!
METRION
AZARATH
POP
RAVEN, YOUR FACE! IT IS CLEAR!
ROOM'S ALL CLEAR OF DEMONS, TOO. TRIGON'S GONE FOR NOW BUT...
...WHAT HAPPENS WHEN YOU GET A TOOTHACHE?
I CAN'T BELIEVE THEY MADE ME A ZIT IN THIS ISSUE!
THIS IS NUTS! I'M GONE!
NO, YOU'RE TRIGON! GET IT!?
KNOT AGAIN!!!
FIN
☺TS3

CREATORS

J. TORRES WRITER

J. Torres won the Shuster Award for Outstanding Writer for his work on Batman: Legends of the Dark Knight, Love As a Foreign Language, and Teen Titans Go! He is also the writer of the Eisner Award-nominated Alison Dare and the YALSA listed Days Like This and Lola: A Ghost Story. Other comic book credits include Avatar: The Last Airbender, Batman: The Brave and the Bold, Legion of Super-Heroes in the 31st Century, Ninja Scroll, Wonder Girl, Wonder Woman, and WALL-E: Recharge.

TIM SMITH 3 ARTIST

Tim Smith 3 has done professional work in illustration and design for over eight years. He uses a mix of traditional and computer techniques and has worked for the following publishers: Marvel, DC Comics, Papercutz, Tokyopop, Archie Comics, and a few others.

GLOSSARY

adolescence (a-dohl-LESS-uhnss)--the period of life during which a child develops into an adult

blemish (BLEHM-ish)--an imperfection on the skin

distracted (dis-STRACT-id)--made someone unable to think or concentrate

hesitated (HEZ-uh-tay-tid)--stopped briefly before doing something because of nervousness or uncertainty about what to do

manifestation (man-uh-fess-TAY-shuhn)--if you manifest something, you create something physical from an emotion or thought

meditating (MED-i-tay-ting)--to spend time in quiet thought for religious purposes or relaxation

remedies (REM-uh-deez)--medicines or treatments that relieve pain or cure what is usually a minor illness

rigorous (RIG-or-uhss)--done carefully and with a lot of attention to detail

vanity (VAN-i-tee)--the quality of people who have too much pride in themselves, especially their appearances

VISUAL QUESTIONS & PROMPTS

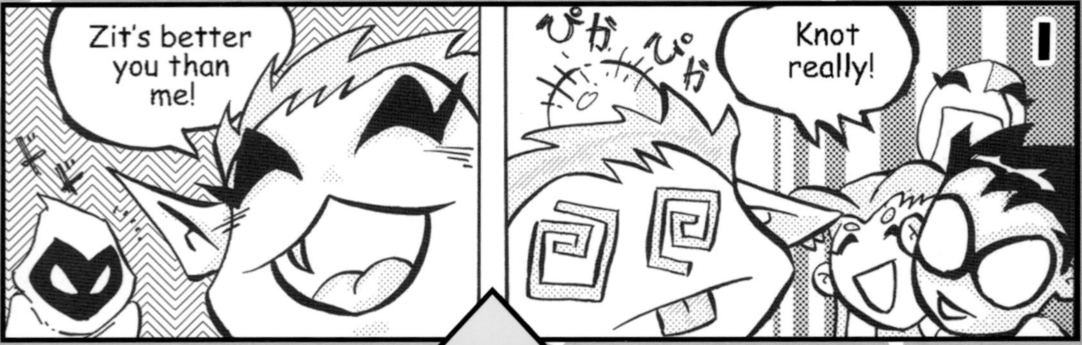
Zit's better you than me!
ぴか ぴか
Knot really!
1

1. What do you think happened between these two panels? Explain your answer.

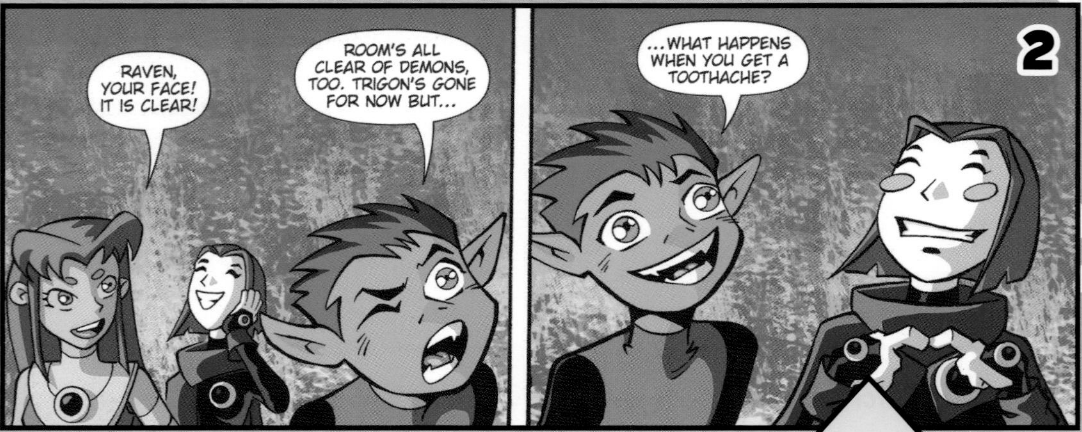
RAVEN, YOUR FACE! IT IS CLEAR!
ROOM'S ALL CLEAR OF DEMONS, TOO. TRIGON'S GONE FOR NOW BUT...
...WHAT HAPPENS WHEN YOU GET A TOOTHACHE?
2

2. Based on Raven's reaction in this panel, what do you think happens when she gets a toothache? Does it become another kind of monster? Write down a few possibilities.

3. Why is there a red highlight around Raven's speech bubble? Why did the comic book's creators do that in this panel?

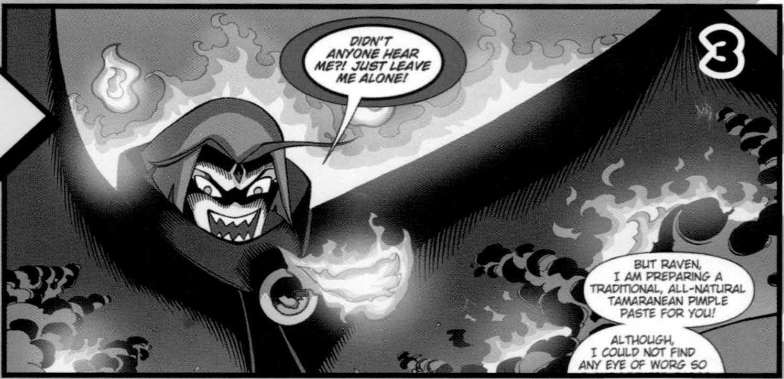
3
DIDN'T ANYONE HEAR ME?! JUST LEAVE ME ALONE!
BUT RAVEN, I AM PREPARING A TRADITIONAL, ALL-NATURAL TAMARANEAN PIMPLE PASTE FOR YOU!
ALTHOUGH, I COULD NOT FIND ANY EYE OF WORG SO

4. Why did the creators of this comic book use red lines behind Raven's head in this panel? How does it make you feel?

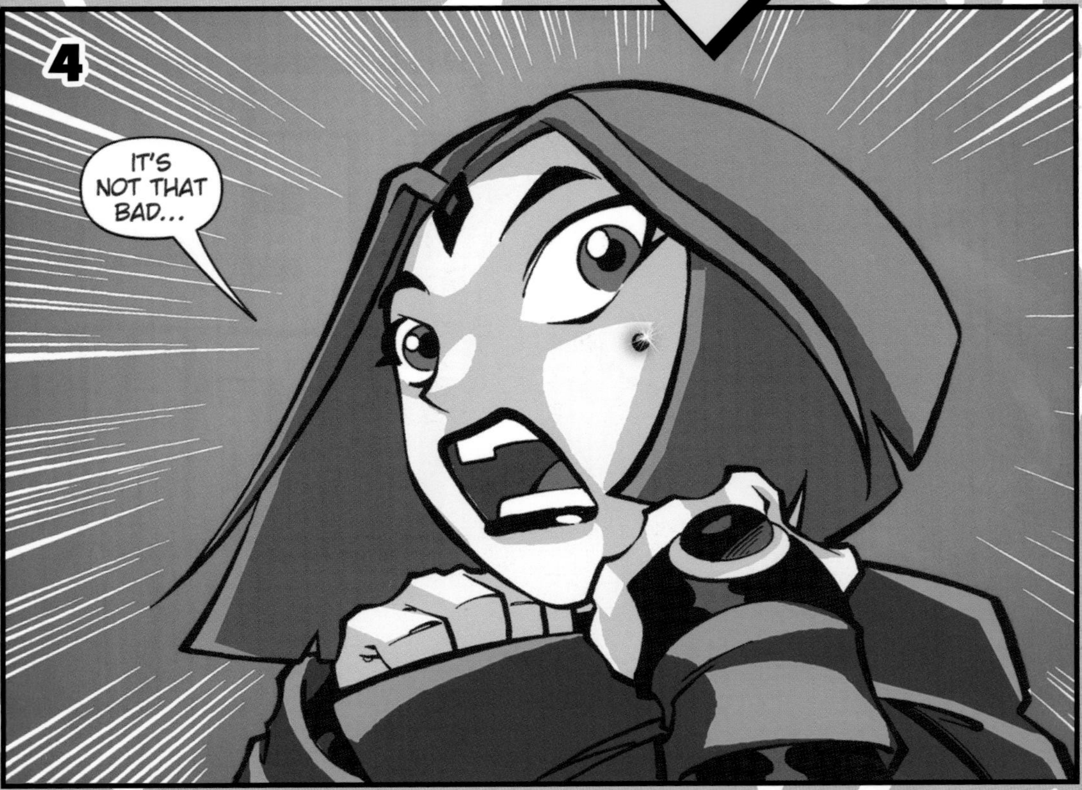
4
IT'S NOT THAT BAD...

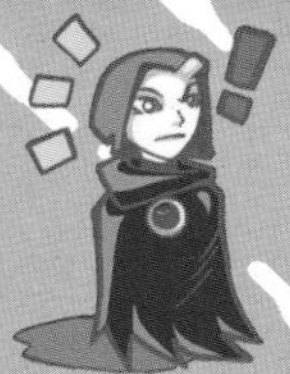

5. Why do you think the young heroes' home base is shaped like a big "T"?

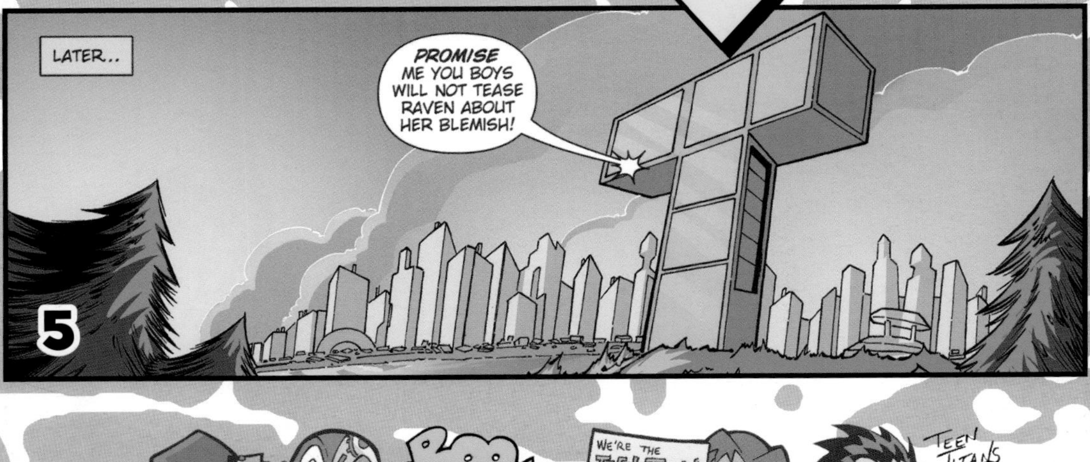
LATER...
PROMISE ME YOU BOYS WILL NOT TEASE RAVEN ABOUT HER BLEMISH!
5

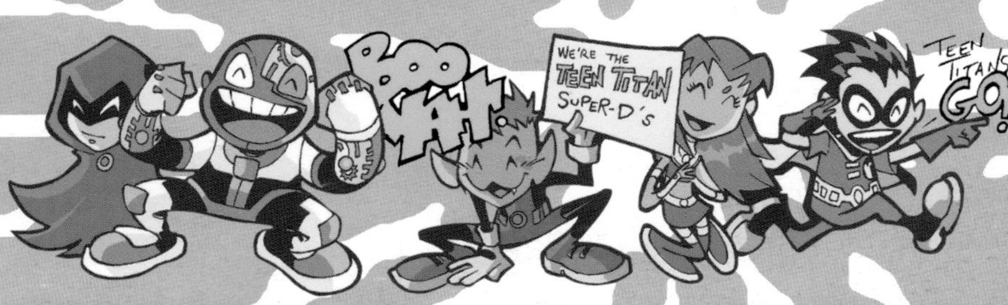
BOOYAH
WE'RE THE TEEN TITAN SUPER-D's
TEEN TITANS GO!

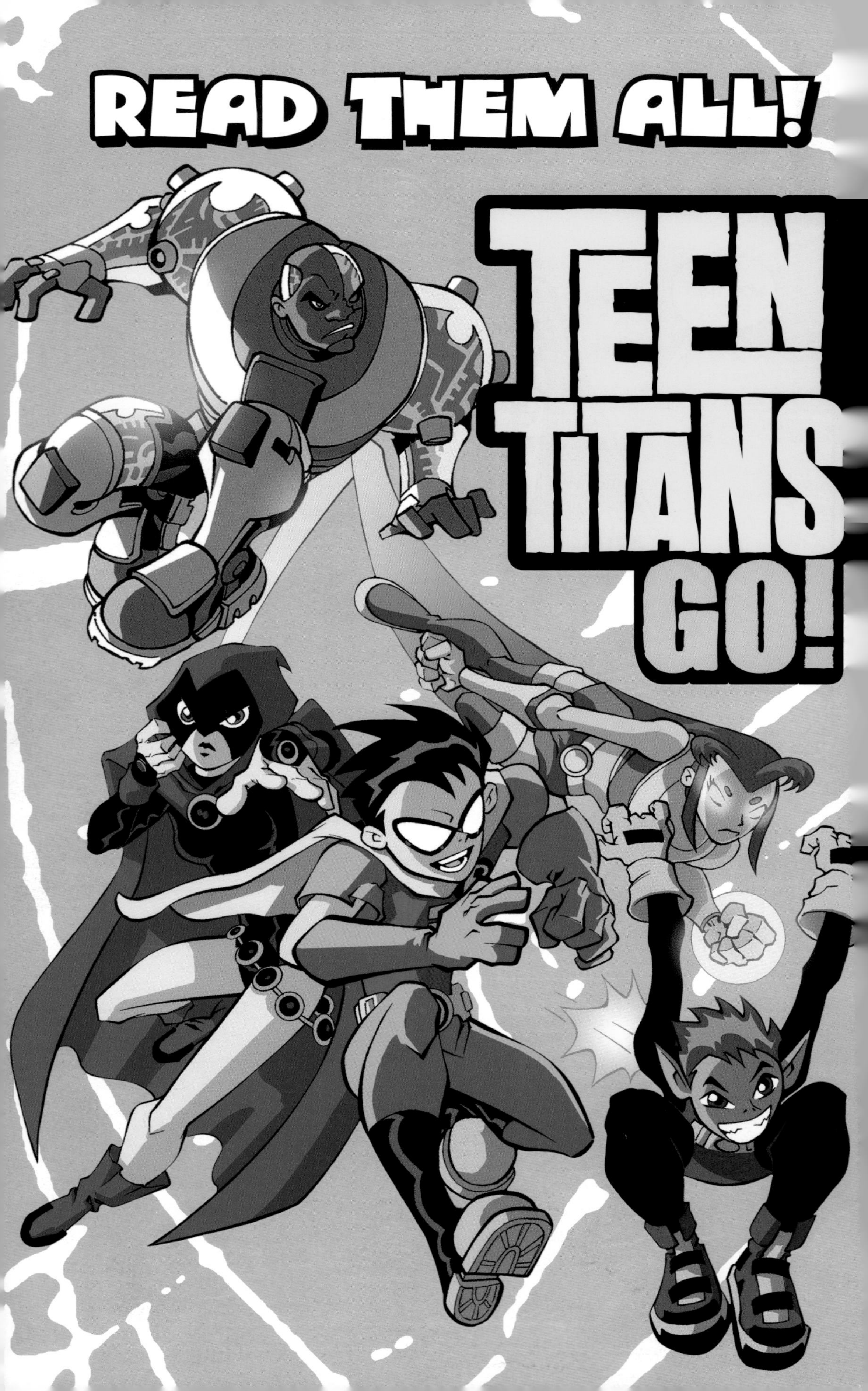
READ THEM ALL!
TEEN TITANS GO!

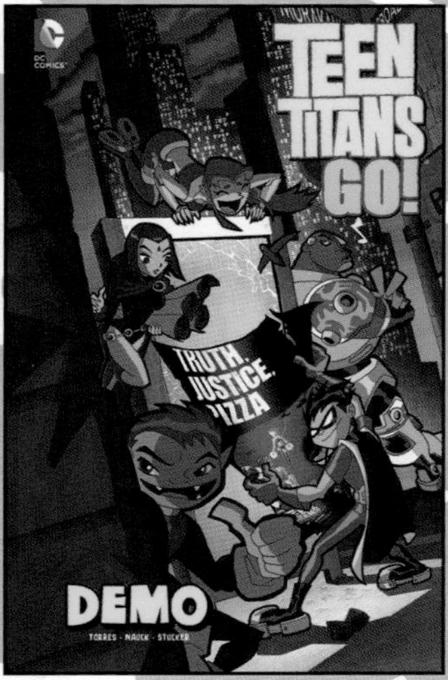
DC COMICS
TEEN TITANS GO!
TRUTH, JUSTICE, PIZZA
DEMO
TORRES · NAUCK · STUCKER

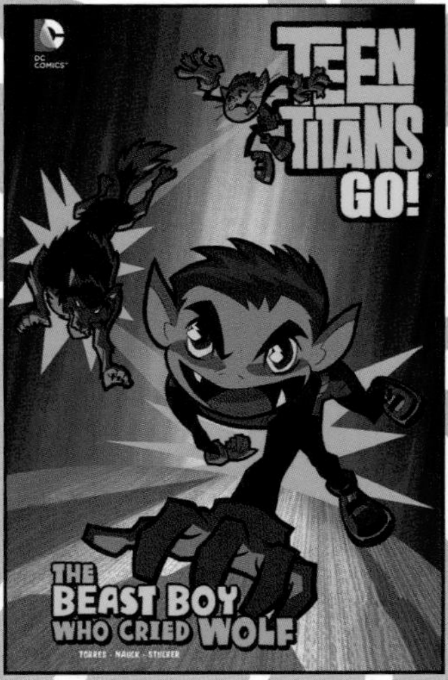
DC COMICS
TEEN TITANS GO!
THE BEAST BOY WHO CRIED WOLF
TORRES · NAUCK · STUCKER

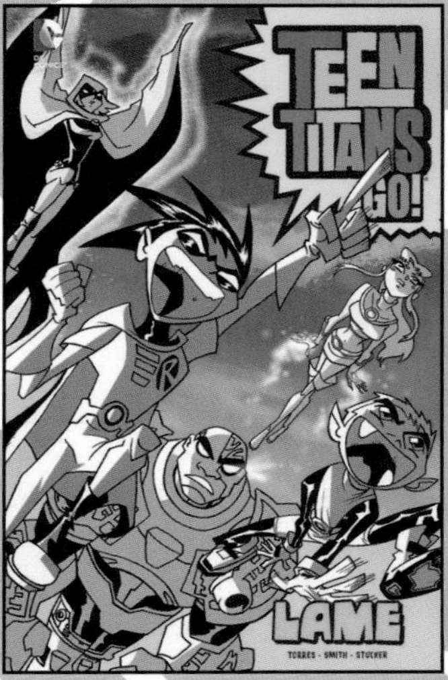
TEEN TITANS GO!
LAME
TORRES · SMITH · STUCKER

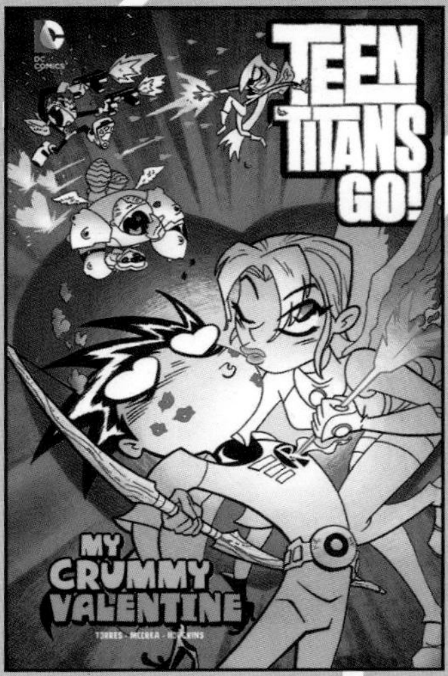
DC COMICS
TEEN TITANS GO!
MY CRUMMY VALENTINE

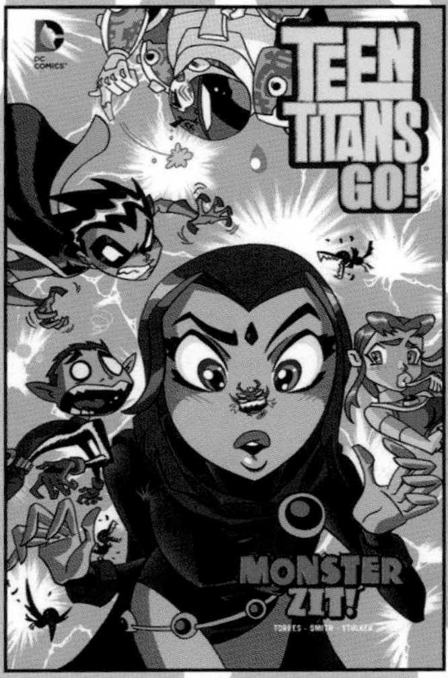
DC COMICS
TEEN TITANS GO!
MONSTER ZIT!
TORRES · SMITH · STUCKER

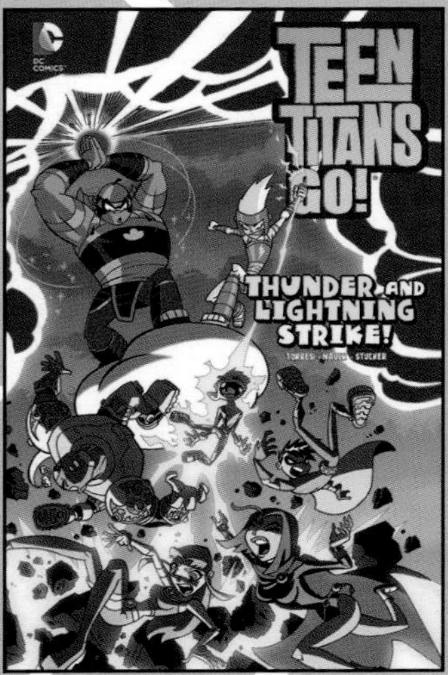
DC COMICS
TEEN TITANS GO!
THUNDER AND LIGHTNING STRIKE!
TORRES · NAUCK · STUCKER

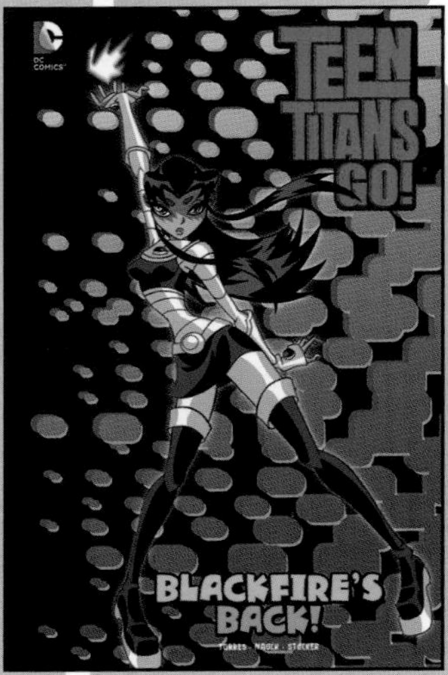
DC COMICS
TEEN TITANS GO!
BLACKFIRE'S BACK!
TORRES · NAUCK · STUCKER

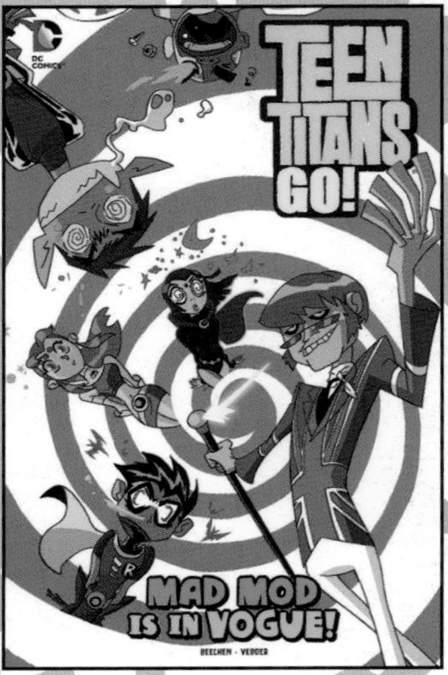
DC COMICS
TEEN TITANS GO!
MAD MOD IS IN VOGUE!
BEECHEN · VEDDER

TEEN TITANS GO!

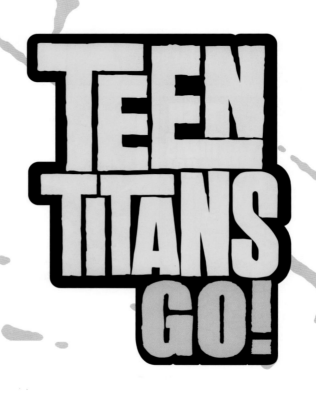